Solo Play

Paxor Seven Book One

Ben Meeks

Sidestreet Publishing

Special Thanks to Jeremiah for introducing me to the LitRPG genre.

PROLOGUE

Tomorrow, Jeremiah Harris will upload and start a new life. He lay in his hospital bed close to death. He spent most of his time asleep now. The kind of sleep that sickness made hard to shake. The plain room was quiet except for the steady beep of the heart monitor. A large vidscreen on the wall opposite the bed had a clock in the top right corner showing the time: 23:57. The vase of flowers his wife had brought wilted on the table beside the bed.

The doctors called it motor neuron disease. While treatment had improved over the years, the end was the same. Jeremiah had lost the use of his legs first, then his arms. Now the only thing keeping him alive was the device on his chest. It was slim and contoured to his body, resembling a piece of black armor. It not only transferred his vitals to the hospital, weak as they were, it controlled his breathing. He had fought a long battle, but the end was in sight. Jeremiah opened his eyes when the nurse on rounds walked into his room.

"How are you feeling?" the nurse asked.

He had no control over his breathing, the machine had taken that from him, but he could speak. His voice was gravely on the exhale, wispy on the inhale.

"Tired," he croaked.

"Tomorrow's the big day. Are you excited?"

He tried to say he was more nervous than excited but lost his strength and slipped into unconsciousness again. The nurse finished her rounds and left the room. The nurse knew he wasn't in good shape, but if he could hold on until tomorrow, he would get a shot at a new life.

His wife, Patty, showed up at seven with a fresh bouquet. She threw out the old flowers and got some fresh water for the vase from the bathroom before putting the flowers in. Patty hadn't slept all night. She was too anxious. Today, her husband would come back to her. They would initiate his upload and in a few days, he would be in the retirement home. He wouldn't be there at home, of course, but he wouldn't be tired and sick either. They could have an actual conversation again. When it was her time, she would join him. They'd been through eighty-three years of marriage, they could make it through a few years of long distance.

Jeremiah opened his eyes at 08:39. He looked to his right and saw the flowers on the table and Patty in the chair.

"There's my girl," he said.

She took his hand and gave him a smile. "How are you feeling?"

"Like a million bucks," he said.

The technician was supposed to come in at nine. There was a knock at the door at nine-fifteen. A man wearing a white coat walked in carrying a tablet.

"All right, let's see here," he said, turning the tablet on. He looked at the screen. "Mr. Harris?"

Patty nodded and dabbed a tear from her eye. "Yes. He's asleep."

"I'm James Graber with Sunrise Uploads." He put all five fingers on the screen and flicked it toward the vid panel on the wall. It turned on and displayed the file. "We have the basic consciousness transferal package. That includes the consciousness upload and transport to..." He paused and scrolled down. "Everafter Retirement Solutions. Is that correct?"

Patty squeezed Jeremiah's hand and nodded. "Yes, we both have spots reserved."

"The way this works is we'll take him to the digitizer. The procedure will take a few hours. We will load his consciousness on a hard drive and send it to the Everafter office in Kenisha. I get asked all the time why we don't send the file FTP. It's an extensive file and we want to make sure there aren't any issues with the transfer. Once there, they'll create his profile and digital body from the pictures and characteristics paperwork you submitted. Do you have any questions before we get started?"

"How long will it take before I can talk to him?"

"The process should take five to seven days."

"Will it hurt?"

"It's completely painless."

Patty shifted in her seat. "What happens to his body?"

"The remains will be cremated," he said, holding out the tablet to her. "I need a few signatures on the red lines."

Patty took the tablet and scrolled down until she had scrawled her name on all the marked sections before handing it back.

She gave his arm a little shake. "Jerry, it's time for your upload."

Jeremiah opened his eyes and gave her a weak smile. "I'm ready."

"Do you want to take a few minutes before we take him back?" Graber asked.

Patty looked back to her husband. He had drifted off again. She leaned forward and kissed him on the forehead. "We're ready now."

Graber opened the door. A couple of people wearing scrubs she hadn't seen around the hospital came in and wheeled him out. Patty sat for a few minutes before heading home, leaving the flowers on the table. Graber followed Jeremiah through the hospital and watched as they strapped him to a table. They put sensors around his head and slid a helmet on top of them. Graber took a disc the size of a briefcase and loaded it into the machine. When he got the all-clear, he started it up. Jeremiah's body spasmed as the consciousness download started. He looked at the screen's progress meter and waited.

When it clicked up to one percent, he opened the tablet again and compared the file number to two stickers he had on hand. The numbers matched. He stuck one to the outside of the case they would transport the disc in. The other should have gone on the front of Jeremiah's disc. Procedure was to label the disc before the upload started. Graber had learned from his years on the job that it was better to wait. If he had to restart the download on a new disc, printing a new sticker was just extra work. He placed the unused sticker in the case. He'd attach it when the download was complete.

Graber went to lunch and spent some time flirting with the nurses. Hours later, when Jeremiah's download finished, he pulled the disc and put it in the case. He didn't put the sticker on the hard drive. He didn't think anything of it. Nothing ever went wrong. He sent the case to the loading dock with the other downloads waiting to be shipped. A few hours later, a drone loaded the hard drives on an automated truck. The truck pulled away on a preset route to Kenisha, taking Jeremiah to his new life.

Chapter One

After what felt like a lifetime, I woke up somewhere other than a hospital bed. The problem was... I wasn't anywhere. I was surrounded by darkness, a disembodied consciousness floating in a void. Something white took shape. It was a body, my body. A milky-looking figure floating in nothing. It wasn't that I was in the body, but I wasn't out of it either. I was simultaneously everything and nothing all at the same time. There wasn't any pain, which was a huge improvement for me, but I didn't feel anything else either. I thought in the virtual afterlife I would have the normal five senses... and a body. Then again, I was out of it when the representative from Everafter Retirement Solutions was talking about the process. Maybe this was a normal transition to the retirement community. They said something about having a digital body created. Patty had submitted pictures. The body that I was supposed to have was from my late thirties. Most of the pictures used were from our trip to the Alaskan Riviera. This didn't seem like a good way to transition someone into a digital afterlife.

Hello? Is anyone there? I tried to speak, but I didn't have a mouth.

A vaguely robotic voice spoke from everywhere.

<Welcome. The upload process is about to begin. Please stand by...>

It was the kind of voice that sounded almost human, human adjacent, but clearly not. The computer must have picked up on my thought patterns. It was good to know I could communicate, even if it was with a program. I didn't feel so helpless. I thought I remembered the rep saying I would have a live person to help me through the onboarding process. He could have bent the truth a little. Maybe there was a clause in the contract that said if all the human representatives were busy, the overflow would go to an automated system. Then they only had to hire one live person part-time and let the AI do the rest. Corps were always bending the rules that way.

Who am I talking to?

<I am the Acuity Gaming Systems artificial intelligence system QD17P3.>

Acuity Gaming Systems? Was that a subsidiary of Ever-after Retirement Solutions?

Is there a live person I can talk to?

<Would you like to load your established profile or start over with character creation?>

Character creation? Does it mean my avatar? Patty handled that already. That must be what it means.

Load the profile.

<Processing... Would you like to play through the tutorial?>

Tutorial? The *What to Expect When You're Uploading* infographic Everafter provided didn't mention anything about a tutorial. Something was off.

I want to talk to someone. Is there a live person I can speak to?

<Would you like to play through the tutorial?>

Live person.

<Would you like to play through—>

No, Customer Service.

<Welcome to Paxor Seven.>

Paxor what?

There was a flash of bright light. As it faded, I began to feel and see. I found myself sitting in a troop transport ship. I had done a stint in the military in my younger years and was familiar with the look of them. This one didn't look quite right. It had the rows of seats split out with two aisles running down the cabin, but it was a little too nice.

The military had always preferred function over aesthetics. This ship looked more like a military-themed cruise liner.

More disconcerting than that was the fact that I was the only person in the cabin. That was weird. How could I be alone here? Acuity was one of the largest retirement solutions on the market, boasting over twelve billion clients. If this was their intake process, I shouldn't be the only one here. This was nothing like what I'd expected.

There was a window in the cabin to my right. Outside, I could see the blackness of space with streaking white lines of hyperspace. That was a dead giveaway I was in a simulation. It was the kind of thing you see in science fiction movies. This was beyond anything possible by current standards. Everafter was supposed to feel real. A relaxing place of recreation and indulgence. All-you-could-eat buffets and afternoon swims. Except for being in a new place, it should be like it was when I was alive. Maybe this was some fancy introduction? Start your new life on a new world? You'd think they would at least mention that in the sales pitch.

What had the AI called it? Paxor Seven? Something was very wrong here. Maybe I was loaded into the wrong system. What if I was lost? Patty could be out there wondering why she hadn't heard from me right now. I tried to get up but was being held in place by a harness. I tried to unhook it, but it wouldn't budge. That's when I noticed my hands. They weren't mine. They were young and strong, attached to muscular arms. I looked at my body. I was fit, fitter than I'd ever been, even in my military days. My belly was flat, even sitting down. The best thing was, I didn't hurt anymore. I'd forgotten what it was like to not be in pain. I felt like a teenager again.

I looked back at the window, this time paying attention to my reflection. A young man looked back at me with a chiseled chin, a full head of hair that was cut short but stylish, and scruff that would almost qualify as a beard. The face in the window looked good, but it didn't look like me, even when I was young. I'd never looked this good. I ran a hand over my head, remembering what a full head of hair felt like. The uniform I wore resembled my uniform in the service, but it had embellishments. Wherever this place was, it felt real, but looked like an imitation.

The ship jolted forward, the stars returning to normal as the ship exited hyperspace. I could see a planet below. It definitely wasn't a planet in our solar system. It had the blues and greens of a living world, but the landmasses didn't match Earth. Above the planet, a large spaceport orbited the planet. It was a large circular structure split into three distinct rings, with a central pillar connecting them. I could see ships coming and going from the planet.

There were two moons that I could see. There could be more on the other side of the planet.

The ship banked to the right and descended toward the planet. As I approached, I could see large landmasses and oceans. As I got closer to the surface, a city came into view. It was split into two sections. The bottom half was rectangular and laid out on a grid. The top was circular, with larger gray buildings that seemed to be oriented around a central building. A wall ran around the entire complex. Its shape reminded me of an ice cream cone.

It looked deserted as I approached. No people, or vehicles, moved around in the streets. Where was everyone? There should be hundreds of thousands of people in Everafter. I didn't expect them all to show up to welcome me, of course, but there should be people around. Something was very wrong here.

The ship descended into the upper section of the city. There were blue banners hanging from almost every building with an image of a shield with a star on the front with four planets circling it resembling a solar system. If it was a solar system, I didn't recognize which one it was. The symbol was like everything else I'd seen; it made no sense.

The ship touched down with the sound of rushing air. My harness unhooked itself at the same time the door in the front of the cabin opened on its own. I sat there waiting for someone to come in and tell me what was going on. Flashing lights running in sequence toward the door appeared on the aisle. It was clear I was supposed to get off. No one was coming. What the hell was going on? Maybe there was someone waiting for me outside who would explain. When I got this whole mess sorted out, I'd have to leave an in-depth review on this whole issue. If they lose a few customers, then so be it. I stood and walked to the end of the aisle, taking a left where a ramp extended to the ground.

I stepped through the hatch onto the ramp and stood in shock at what I saw. At the bottom of the ramp, five people in military garb stood in front of the ship. Their uniforms matched what I was wearing. Two guards stood on either side of… I didn't know what it was. Some kind of lizard person. Its skin was dark gray with black spots with a glossy sheen, as if it were wet. It had a large mouth, two round black eyes, and something dark purple that didn't quite look like hair draped down the back of its head. It wore the same uniform as the other Marines and clearly was important, judging by the way they deferred to it. A higher rank, I suppose. I walked down the ramp. When I got to the bottom, the thing started talking.

"Welcome to Port Bax, Marines. I'm Colonel Radim. The separatist rebellion has already claimed half the planet and is gaining momentum. It's our job to put down that rebellion. Outside of these walls, you'll find a hostile world. The danger of predatory wildlife is only surpassed by a group of indigenous humanoids called the Pangol. Do not underestimate them. Work together with your fellow Marines to complete your missions. You don't want to be on your own here. If you go it alone, you'll end up dead. I'll be the one sending condolence vids to your families. Do *not* make more work for me." The lizard-thing shifted on his weight, looking around the empty hangar. "Grab your gear and report to headquarters to get your assignments."

With that, the group turned and exited the hangar through a gate to my right, leaving me standing alone with no idea what to do next.

Chapter Two

Sparkling blue lights on the ground to my right caught my attention. A metal disc resembling an upside-down bowl materialized out of the light beside me. A section of the dome separated and raised, revealing a camera. The camera looked around for a moment before four spider-like legs unfolded from underneath and it stood up. It was a robot about the size of a house cat. It stood beside me, shuffling like it was waiting for something. That was weird, but no weirder than the alien in a military uniform welcoming me to a starport I didn't know I was going to.

I looked back at the ship. A platform loaded with gear had descended from the bottom. A few Marines stood around the platform but didn't appear to be doing anything while another pulled a conveyor belt over. When it was in place, they started unloading. I moved toward them. The robot followed me, keeping pace. I stopped and turned around. It stopped right beside me. I walked in a large circle. It walked in a smaller circle beside me. I didn't know why it was following me, but I wanted it to stop.

I pointed at nothing. "What's that, over there?"

Its camera turned to see what I was pointing at. I sprinted to the Marines under the ship, leaving it behind.

"Could you tell me where I am?" I said as the robot ran up beside me.

"Can't talk now. Have to unload the cargo," one Marine said. "Sergeant Hopkins can tell you where you need to be."

"Where might I find him?"

The Marine pointed across the hangar bay to a man standing by the gate. I crossed the bay; the robot kept pace. He had sergeant's bars on his uniform so this had to be the guy.

"Excuse me... Sergeant Hopkins? Hi," I said. "I need some help. I—"

"Your momma can't help you on Paxor Seven. Now grab your gear."

"I think there's some kind of mistake. I think I'm in the wrong place."

He stuck his chin out at me. "And why would you think that?"

"I'm not supposed to be here."

"Pray tell, where do you think you should be?"

"Everafter. You see—"

"You prayin' for death? 'Cause there's plenty to go around on Paxor Seven."

"No, you don't understand."

"Oh, I get it. You're one of them contentious objectors. This is a fine sight. The corps must be scraping the bottom of the barrel if the best they can muster is a fraggin' pacifist. I promise you the separatists don't care about your gentle character. They're gonna rip out your soft little spine and use it for a barrel brush."

"Umm... Okay."

He placed his hands on his hips. "The only chance you got is to stick with your squad and kill the enemy before they kill you."

This was clearly going nowhere. Maybe I could find a phone or a computer I could send a message from. I headed for the door.

The sergeant slapped a hand on my chest. "You can't go without your gear. Not that it will make much of a difference for a tender belly like you."

I sighed. "Where do I get my gear from?"

He pulled a hand off my chest and pointed two fingers at the Marines standing by the ship on the other side of the hangar. I turned and walked back. They had unloaded a single duffle bag and were standing behind it. I picked it up. It must be for me, it was the only bag, and I was the only one here. I picked it up and headed for the door.

The sergeant scowled as I approached. I gave the sergeant a little smile and gave the bag a shake as I passed him.

He stopped me again. "Outside this door, you need to be ready for a fight. Better gear up. You're gonna need all the help you can get."

I was getting tired of all the hoops I had to jump through, but if it got me somewhere I could get some help, it would be worth it. I dropped the bag and opened the zipper. There was a pile of gear inside. I pulled out a tactical belt with an assortment of pouches. It had a holster with a leg strap on one side. I put it on, taking a minute to get a comfortable fit. Next, I pulled out a backpack that matched the camo pattern of my uniform. Standard military issue with a molle system that they quit using over a thousand years ago in favor of the magtech system. I didn't understand why the equipment was so out of date. I pulled a big revolver out of the bag, turning it over in my hands. It was matte black with polymer grips with a satisfying heft in the hand. No surprise it was a perfect fit in the holster.

Next was a kind of headpiece. It had a microphone, earpiece, and a screen that fit over my left eye. When I got it into position, a display popped up. It looked similar to the role-playing games I used to play when I was young. At the top left, the name Specter was listed. I wasn't sure what was below it. It had my picture in a circular frame. Well, not my picture, but what I looked like here. There were four different colored bars wrapping around the picture. The outermost bar was red, then yellow, blue, and the innermost bar was green. The yellow bar was down by a quarter. I didn't know what that meant. I focused on the circle and a popup appeared.

<Player Multimeter:>

<The multimeter displays the player's health(red), energy(yellow), psyche(blue), and hunger(green).>

A second multimeter was below the first, labeled Service Drone. It had a picture of the robot that had been following me around. It was identical to mine except missing the green bar. When my attention shifted away from the multimeter, the popup disappeared. I had a map on the top right. I could see the layout of the hangar and the ship. A green dot clearly represented my position. A second marked the service drone beside me. On the bottom left, a holographic screen popped up with a message.

<Welcome to Paxor 7>

<Achievement: Tip of the Spear>

<You are the first player to log in to Paxor Seven. You have received the title "the First.">

The name above the multimeter changed to "Specter the First."

The first *player* to log in… So, did that mean I really was the only person here? Where was *here* anyway? I'd never heard of a game called Paxor Seven. There had to be some kind of mix-up. I just needed to find some way to contact Patty. Then we could sort it all out together.

I turned to the sergeant. "Well?"

"That's not everything."

I looked at the bag on the ground. I didn't see anything else in it. Bending down, I felt around and found an envelope inside. I shoved it in a pocket without looking at it. When I pulled it out, the bag disappeared into light blue pixels. A new message displayed though the eye piece.

<Mission complete: Gear up>

<Rewards:>

<100 Experience>

<Starting Gear>

<Continue>

I looked at the continue button, wondering how to press it. As I looked at it, it clicked and the message updated.

<Mission: Report to HQ>

<Go to headquarters to receive your brigade assignment.>

<Reward: 50 Experience>

<Accept - Reject>

I had no intention of playing this game. I just needed to talk to a real person. The message was transparent in my vision so I could look at it or look through it. It was a little distracting, but I ignored it.

I held my arms out to my sides, presenting myself to the sergeant for inspection.

"Stay safe out there, pacifist," the sergeant grunted.

I stepped through the doors into a military base. To my left, there was a courtyard with five buildings around it. The one in the middle had a sign, Pour Decisions—Enlisted Club. There were two buildings on either side of it. They were marked as Third Brigade with a banner of a mountain, Fourth Brigade with a four-leaf clover, Eighth Brigade with an ankh, and Eleventh with the number eleven.

I spotted a woman in military uniform walking by. "Excuse me, I need some help."

She stopped walking and turned to me. "If you've just landed, you should report to headquarters to be assigned to a brigade."

"Right, I know about that. I need to make a call. Is there a phone I could use or something?"

She looked puzzled by the question. "You can communicate through your heads-up display to anyone on the planet if you know their call sign."

"I need to call my wife in the real world. Is there a way I can do that?"

"You mean... Earth?"

"Yes, she lives on Earth," I said.

"Well, until they develop faster-than-light communications, the quickest way to get a message to Earth is to send a recording on the next transport ship. You'd probably die of old age before you got a reply to a call as far out as we are."

"Too late," I said.

"What do you mean?"

"Nothing. Thanks for your help."

I don't know why I thought a non-player character could help me with anything relating to outside the game, but it was worth a shot. Time for Plan B. I'd have to find another player and get them to contact someone for me. The achievement said I was the first player in the game, though. Maybe there was a way to contact customer service. If not, I'd just have to wait until someone else showed up.

Chapter Three

I stood in the street for a few minutes, looking at the mission, with the service drone shuffling in the dirt beside me. Patty was probably at home wringing her hands, wondering what had happened to me. I needed a distraction. The only distraction available was the game. I didn't like the idea of playing a game while Patty was sitting home worried sick, but there was nothing else I could do. I resolved to play until I found someone I could convince to reach out to her. As soon as she found out what happened to me, she could get me where I was supposed to be. I had to play, but I promised myself I wouldn't have any fun. It didn't feel right. I focused on Accept. It clicked, and the screen disappeared.

I looked down at the service drone. "Don't suppose you know where headquarters is?"

"Accessing navigation system," it said. "Marking location, headquarters, on minimap."

"Oh, you can talk. What systems do you have equipped?"

The drone's camera wiggled. "Listing systems... Navigation... End list."

I looked at the map. A yellow dot appeared on a group of buildings ahead of me. I walked past the barracks and another building with a sign designating it as the training facility. I found headquarters in the middle of the next group of buildings. There were two Marines guarding the door. They were huge, with muscles that looked like they would burst the seams of their uniforms at any second. Each soldier was holding a vicious looking machine gun. They didn't seem to notice I was there. I walked up to the building wondering if they would stop me, but they didn't pay any attention to me as I walked inside.

When I walked inside, a man sitting behind a desk looked up from a computer. "What can I do for you, Marine?"

"I'm here to get my brigade assignment," I said.

"Terminal on the wall," he said, pointing to a computer bank on the left wall.

I walked over to one. The screen flickered to life as I approached.

<Choose a Brigade>

<Brigades are a player faction. Factions compete for honor and in-game rewards.>

<The factions are:>

<Third Brigade>

<Fourth Brigade>

<Eighth Brigade>

<Eleventh Brigade>

There were pictures associated with each brigade. The third was a mountain, the fourth was a four-leaf clover, the eighth was an ankh, and the eleventh was the number eleven.

I didn't have strong feelings about which brigade to join. I wasn't planning to be around long enough for it to make a difference. Eleventh was the lowest on the list, making it closest to the accept button. I selected Eleventh and accepted it. An insignia appeared on the left shoulder of my uniform. It was a circle with a white number eleven on a blue background.

<Mission Complete: Report to HQ>

<Faction Selected: Eleventh Brigade>

<Reward: 50 Experience>

<Mission: Settling In>

<Locate and Set Up Your Locker in the Barracks>

<Rewards: 25 Experience>

<Accept - Reject>

I accepted the mission. A second appeared right after it.

<Mission: Get Your Bearings>

<Familiarize Yourself with Port Bax>

<Speak to Cassandra at the Drone Warehouse>

<Speak to Silas at the Weapons Boutique>

<Speak to Boris at the Armor Emporium>

<Speak to Doctor Silvers at the Medical Treatment Center>

<Speak to Parson at the Enlisted Club>

<Reward: 600 Experience>

<Accept - Reject>

I accepted this one too. I exited headquarters and looked around. There were a lot of options on what to do next. One thing on the list stood out to me. The Drone Warehouse. I bet I could find out why this robot was following me around.

"Service drone, mark Drone Warehouse on the map… please," I said.

I don't know why I said please. It was a robot in a game. I guess if it was helping me, some manners weren't too much to ask. I was probably being stupid.

"Marking location, Drone Warehouse, on minimap."

A green dot appeared on the border of my map. It must be farther away than the area shown on my map. I walked toward the dot, coming to a wall with a gate large enough to drive two cars through. A sign on the gate read Civilian District. On the other side of the gate, I looked back to a sign that read Military District. Port Bax seemed to be split in half with this gate allowing access between them. This must be the border between the round section and the rectangular section I had seen from the air.

The buildings in the civilian district were laid out on a grid. They were made of stacked rectangular stones. While they all looked the same, they weren't all identical. Some were two stories with doors and windows in different configurations. The banners that were common in the military district were missing here. A few people walked through the streets, but the town seemed mostly deserted. I walked down the street, heading for the yellow circle. I rounded a corner and spotted the Drone Warehouse. A woman was standing in front of it. She wore a gray shirt with the sleeves rolled up and matching pants. She had a leather apron tied around her waist and goggles on her head.

"Are you Cassandra?" I asked.

"I am," she said, pulling the goggles up to her forehead. She had a line of grime on her face outlining where the goggles had been. "What can I do for you?"

<Mission: Get Your Bearings>

<Speak to Cassandra at the Drone Warehouse: Complete>

"I wanted to get some information about drones."

She shot me a smile. "Well, this is the place. What did you want to know?"

"What does a service drone do exactly?"

"It serves its owner. It can do all kinds of menial tasks."

"So… it's a robot butler?"

"You could say that," she said. "You can equip them with gear to assist you with your missions. I'd show you some options, but I'm having a problem with the shop right now. If you have a few minutes to spare, maybe you could help me?"

That explained why it was following me around. I guess it was nice to have something helping me out. It had come in handy finding the Drone Warehouse; a few of those upgrades could come in handy.

"Sure, what's the problem?"

"I've got a sarloc infestation in my basement. They're getting in my parts and chewing cables, just making a mess of things. I don't want to go inside with them down there. They freak me out. Could you go down to the basement and set some traps for me? If you could grab some Low Flow Injectors while you're down there, it would be a big help."

<Mission: Pest Control>

<Set 4 Sarloc Traps in the basement of the Drone Warehouse.>

<Bonus objective: Return 4 Low Flow Injectors to Cassandra at the Drone Warehouse.>

<Reward:>

<150 Experience>

<50 Reputation: Port Bax Shopkeepers Union>

<25 Credits>

<Accept - Reject>

I accepted the mission.

"What is a sarloc exactly?"

"They started out as rats that hitched a ride on the terraforming ships. Over time, they evolved into something else."

I stepped past her into the shop. "I'll take a look."

"You'll find the traps behind the counter," she said, leaning into the doorway.

The service drone followed close behind as I moved through the shop. The shelves stored all kinds of mechanical parts and gadgets I didn't recognize. To the left of the counter, I passed a contraption that looked like a large metal fireplace. Behind the counter, I found the traps. They were easy to spot. The traps had a glow to them that made them stand out. They were large discs about a foot in diameter with a button on one side. I picked them up. They had a domed top that made them hard to hold. Maybe I could put them in my backpack until I needed them. I set the discs on the counter and reached back to take off my backpack. When I touched it, an inventory menu popped up.

My backpack had fifteen empty slots. I wondered if I could get these discs into my inventory without taking my backpack off. It made sense in a game with an inventory menu. I picked up one disc and waved it in the air behind one of the empty backpack slots. Nothing happened. I had the feeling someone was watching me. I looked down at my service drone, then over to the door. Cassandra was looking at me through the door. I shot her an awkward smile and lowered the disc with it tucked against my arm in a vain attempt to hide it. It touched my backpack and disappeared from my hand, appearing in the first inventory slot.

I picked up the discs and touched them to my backpack. They appeared in my inventory in a single stack of four. Now I just had to figure out how to take them out. I concentrated on the stack. The number shifted from four to three, and one re-materialized in my hand. Easy enough. Another tap on my backpack closed the inventory menu.

I found a trapdoor in the floor behind the counter. Pulling it open revealed stairs descending into darkness to the basement. I didn't see any light switches.

"Service drone." I paused thinking how annoying it would be to keep referring to my robot as "service drone." It needed a name. Patty had a cat that used to follow me around named Buttons because it had a couple white spots on its chest that looked like buttons of a tuxedo. That would do.

"I'm going to call you Buttons. Any problem with that?"

"Negative. Personal designation has been changed to Buttons."

The name above the robot's multimeter changed from Service Drone to Buttons.

"Buttons, can you tell me where a light switch for the basement is?"

The robot shuffled in place. "Function unavailable, systems scanner is not equipped."

Chapter Four

I eased down the stairs into the dark, feeling the walls as I went. It was almost pitch black by the time I made it to the bottom of the stairs. The service drone clattered its way down the stairs behind me. I ran my hands over the wall on the way down the stairs and finally felt a switch at the bottom. I caught sight of a pair of eyes watching me and I paused with my hand on the switch. They glowed in the dark, reflecting what little light was spilling in from upstairs. I stood watching the eyes. Something scurried off to my right, making me jump. I pressed the switch. The lights flickered, giving me a glimpse of something that scuttled off before they powered up. When they came on they weren't bright, just enough, really, to see without running into anything.

The basement was the same size as the shop above. Shelves full of boxes lined the walls with additional rows of shelving in the middle. There were two lights in the ceiling that lit up the center of the room. If there was nothing in the room, they might have been sufficient. As it was, they left the walls dim. I could hear scratching and scurrying from somewhere farther in. There were two glowing circles in corners of the room to my left and right. They were the same size as the traps, so that must be where I was supposed to set them.

"Service drone, Buttons, can you scan for sarlocs or something?"

Its camera wiggled a little from side to side. "Function unavailable, bio scanner is not equipped."

"Ah, okay then," I said. "We'll do it the old-fashioned way."

I moved to the circle on the right, keeping an eye out for sarlocs. The eyes I saw must have belonged to a sarloc, but I hadn't gotten a good enough look at it to know what to expect. The coast looked clear. I knelt beside the glowing ring. A box on the shelf beside the circle shuddered. I paused, watching the box. A scratching sound came from inside it. I sat still, waiting to see if something was going to jump out at me. The box continued to shudder and scratch, but nothing came out. I eased forward, placing the trap in the circle and... nothing happened. I expected to get a notification, or for the glowing spot on the floor to go away. Something wasn't right. That's when I remembered the button. I pressed it.

<Sarloc Trap Armed>

<Mission: Pest Control>

<Objective: Set Sarloc Traps 1/4>

"Okay, no problem," I muttered to myself.

I looked at the box. If I was going to play the game, I might as well do it right. I drew my pistol and paused. I wasn't sure how Cassandra would take gunfire in her basement. She did say the sarlocs were destroying everything down here though, so maybe it would be all right. I caught myself in this line of thought and felt a little silly. This was a military-based game with guns everywhere. Why would shooting be a problem?

I pointed the pistol at the box, took a step forward, and kicked it with my foot. It tipped over on the floor. The box was still for a second before a creature popped out. It looked like a hairless opossum with beady red eyes and fangs. It turned toward me and screeched. I fired. The bullet hit the floor beside it, leaving a gouge in the concrete. It charged me, snapping at my feet. I tried to move out of the way but was too slow. I felt the teeth sink into my boot and a tingle and pressure in my foot. It wasn't pain I felt, it was the simulation of a pain response.

I fired and missed again. How could I be missing from three feet away? It crawled up my boot and bit into my leg. I tried to kick it away but couldn't get it off. After two bites, my red health bar dropped from one hundred to sixty-four life. I put my revolver a foot away and fired again. This time I hit it. That must be the trick, point-blank range. I held the gun close, fired, and missed again. The bullet seemed to just go straight through it. The sarloc clenched its jaws, driving its teeth deeper into my leg. Buttons was just standing there watching me get chewed to pieces.

"Help me!" I shouted.

"Unable to comply," it said. "No combat capabilities available."

"Then stand on the sarloc," I commanded.

Buttons walked over and climbed on top of the creature. The sarloc let go of me and twisted around to attack the service drone. The drone's health bar started falling, but it gave me time to breathe. I fired two more shots while the sarloc focused on the drone and hit with one of them. I took my time aiming down the sights, resolving not to miss again. When the sights lined up, I squeezed the trigger. *Click.*

I'd run out of ammo. How did I reload? The pistol was modeled after real firearms, so reloading shouldn't be difficult. I found a button on the side and pressed it. The cylinder ejected from the side of the gun. It fell to the floor and rolled under a shelf. I hoped I wouldn't need it.

Shoving a hand into my ammo pouch, I felt something round. I pulled it out to discover a new cylinder with ammo already loaded. I tried to put it in the gun, but it didn't go. It looked like it should fit, but something was stopping it. A quick inspection of the cylinder revealed the problem. There was a knob on one side with arrows pointing in its direction. It was backward. I flipped it around and slammed it into the revolver. I fired all six shots as fast as I could, missing with more than I hit, but it was enough. The sarloc fell to the ground and didn't move.

Buttons shambled to its normal spot beside me. Its health bar showed seventeen percent. It wasn't moving as smoothly. It had a shudder that wasn't there before, with the occasional spark shooting out from his camera.

The sarloc's body was glowing the same as the circle for the sarloc traps. For all I knew, it could be healing and would jump and attack me again. I gave it a little nudge with my foot to make sure it was dead, and a window popped up.

<You have Received 2 Credits>

<You Can Loot the Following:>

<Small Feather>

<Corroded Metal Vest>

<Loot All - Abandon>

I didn't know what a small feather was used for or where the sarloc had been hiding a metal vest. I'd learned from the games I'd played that you don't turn down loot, especially at the beginning. I could select individual items to loot, but selected Loot All instead.

The feather and metal vest went into my inventory. The sarloc's body disintegrated into blue pixels. I'd lost about two-thirds of my life from this little skirmish. I was wholly unprepared for a fight. The sarloc had been hard to hit, too hard. Something didn't seem right. If this was an entry level monster, then I shouldn't have much trouble fighting it. Maybe the corroded metal vest would at least give me a little more protection.

I touched my backpack to open my inventory and selected the vest.

<You do not have the required skill to use this item.>

It wasn't going to help after all. Nothing I could do but keep moving. I could see a new glowing spot on the floor in the far corner. It looked like one trap went in each corner of the basement. Easy enough. I didn't want to tangle with any more sarlocs. The first one did a number on Buttons and me. I wasn't sure we would survive another one. I had placed one trap and almost been killed but I hadn't seen any of the injectors I was supposed to get. Maybe I could complete the mission without fighting any more sarlocs.

A quick circle around the room to check the shelves and place the traps should do the trick.

I moved with my pistol ready, scanning the shelves and noticed a crate. It differed from everything else I saw. The shelves were full of cardboard boxes with labels of technical data. The crate was polished metal and seemed to be well put together. Everything on the shelves had been jumbled together. The crate was on its own, with space between it and the other boxes. I walked over and opened the lid.

<You Can Loot the Following:>

<Corroded Metal Gloves>

<Corroded Armor Plating>

<Low Flow Injector>

<Loot All - Abandon>

I selected Loot All.

<Bonus Objective: Low Flow Injectors: 1/4>

Now I knew what to look for. All I had to do was place the traps, find a few more crates, and avoid sarlocs. Should be easy enough. I turned to set the next trap and stopped short when I spotted two sets of glowing red eyes ahead. Two sarlocs were chewing on something close to the glowing disc. One by itself had just about killed me. Two at the same time was a big nope for me. I could set the trap by the stairs and see if they'd moved on when I finished. I turned and walked toward the stairs and noticed that, for once, my drone wasn't following me. Buttons was moving toward the sarlocs. It was a quarter of the way across the room before I could do anything.

"Hey, what are you doing?" I asked.

"Fulfilling operator command, stand on sarlocs," it said.

"No! Cancel... Come back!"

Buttons stopped and turned around, but it was too late. It had gotten the sarlocs' attention. They charged. I aimed the pistol and fired. At least, I tried to. I'd forgotten to reload. The revolver was much easier to reload the second time. I barely fumbled with it at all, but before I finished, the sarlocs had caught up to my drone and attacked. They jumped on Buttons, biting and clawing in a vicious attack. I fired, the bullet going high. They tore into my service drone, making quick work of it. I watched its life bar plummet to zero.

I fired the remaining five rounds, hitting with three of them. Was it luck or was I getting used to the pistol? I ejected the cylinder and pulled a new one from my ammo pouch. I got this one in much faster, but not before the sarlocs were on top of me. One went after my leg while the other leapt onto me, biting my chest. My health bar was falling fast. I put the revolver up against the one on my chest and fired as fast as I could, only managing one hit at point-blank range. It was enough to kill the sarloc, but not enough to save me. My health bar hit zero and everything went black.

Chapter Five

<You have been killed.>

<You have been resurrected with 10% Life and Energy. All items have lost 50% Durability.>

I came to lying on my back in a big glass tube. I felt all right for having died… again. The tube slid down with the sound of swooshing air from a pressure change. I eased up into a sitting position. My uniform was torn and dirty. It didn't look like the damage had come from the sarloc attack, it just looked old and dingy. The red and yellow bars of my multimeter sat at a sliver. My yellow energy bar started moving up slowly.

A woman in a white coat walked over to me. "Good to see you awake. It was touch and go there for a minute."

"Where am I?"

"I'm Doctor Silvers and this is the Medical Treatment Center in Port Bax. You're free to go, but I recommend further treatment before you do."

<Mission: Get Your Bearings>

<Mission Objective: Speak to Doctor Silvers at the Medical Treatment Center: Complete>

"What kind of treatment?"

She flashed me a smile. "There's only one treatment here. The express cellular regeneration module. ECR, for short. There's a nominal fee for treatment, of course."

"Of course," I said. "How nominal are we talking?"

"It depends on the level of treatment needed," she said. "If you'll follow me, we'll devise a treatment plan."

I eased off the table and followed her into another room. For the first time since I stepped off the shuttle, I didn't see Buttons. The walls were lined with more glass tubes, though these were mounted vertically. Doctor Silvers walked to the closest one and hit a button. The tube rotated, revealing an opening large enough to step through.

"You're not claustrophobic, are you?"

I stepped into the tube. "I don't think so."

She tapped away on the control panel. It rotated back into position around me. "This will only take a second."

The machine started whirring. With the confined space and the noise, I could see how someone could get anxious inside it. A disc of light appeared above my head at the top of the tube. It moved down across my body to my feet, then reversed direction, moving back up over my head.

Doctor Silvers looked at the display. "Full regeneration will cost twelve credits. Should I proceed?"

"Yes, please."

I was expecting more than twelve credits. That seemed like nothing to heal from ten percent health to full. She typed on the display and a warbling hum emanated from the machine. A blue light appeared at the top of the tube and moved down slowly. It looked like the blue pixels I had seen items materialize from. I felt a warm tingling sensation on my skin. I watched my health bar as the light moved over me. The red part of the bar that was only a sliver moved up slowly, reaching 100% by the time it got to my feet. The humming stopped, and the tube slid open.

"How are you feeling?" Silvers asked as I stepped out of the tube.

"Good as new," I said. "I don't suppose you have a portable ERC?"

Silvers chuckled. "ECR, and no. We use nanobots for injuries in the field. Are you familiar with nanobots?"

I nodded. "I know the concept. Tiny robots that got their name because they're the size of a nanometer, right?"

"That's correct! They're preprogrammed and loaded into medsticks. We have them for sale if you need some for your next outing."

"Thanks, I'll definitely need to gear up. How much are they?"

She opened a cabinet and pulled out a white rectangular box six inches long and two inches wide. She walked over and showed it to me. It had a red medical cross surrounded by a circle on one side. A black iris protruded slightly from one end with a matching button opposite the cross.

"All you do is place the iris against your skin and press the button," Silvers said, acting it out as she spoke. "They have five uses before the nanobots are depleted and cost twenty-five credits per unit."

"Let me figure out what else I need," I said, "and I'll let you know, okay? I might be a little short."

She smiled. "No problem. I'll be here if you need anything."

I walked out of the hospital and into the military district. A man materialized in front of me that didn't look like part of the game. Instead of a uniform, he looked like he was dressed for the office. Business casual. The tablet in his hands looked modern, not something from the game. He looked around, getting his bearings. Finally, I'd found someone that might be able to help me.

"Excuse me, I think I'm lost," I said. "I'm not supposed to be here."

He looked at me and then down at the tablet, his brow furrowing with confusion.

"Excuse me," I said, waving a hand in his direction.

He paused and looked up at me from the tablet.

"I need to get in contact with my wife. I'm not supposed to be here."

"That's a strange mission line," he mumbled.

"It's not a mission line, I need your help," I said, trying to grab the tablet away from him. My hand went right through it.

He touched a finger to his headset. "Tammy, I found the anomaly. It's a non-player character that seems to be operating independently... I know that's impossible, that's why I called you."

"I'm not an NPC," I said. "Now hang up on Tammy and talk to me."

"Let me call you back." He turned to me, looking skeptical. "Who's the president?"

"What the hell difference does it make?"

"Just answer the question," he said.

I sighed. "Ahmed Khouri."

"You aren't an NPC... If you were, you would have given me the name of the president of the Federation... but you can't be a player because the game doesn't go live for another twelve hours. You can't be an AI because you don't know who the president is... So, what are you? Some kind of virus?"

"What do you mean I don't know who the president is? Khouri just started his term two months ago. I voted for him."

He looked skeptical. "Khouri's term ended. Jabari Okeke is the president now."

I raised a hand to my forehead. "Okeke? The Director of Interplanetary Intellect?"

"He used to be... Before he became president of the colonies," the man said. "If you're a player, then what's your account number?"

"I'm not a player. I'm just... here. I don't know how I got here. My name is Jeremiah Harris."

He typed on his tablet. "There's no account registered under that name. I need to get your account ID."

I sighed. "I don't have an account ID."

"Hang on." He waved the tablet in front of me as if he were doing a scan.

"What's your name?" I asked.

"Faizal... Oh my God, you're a player. I see you logged in. You didn't hack in... There's no outside connection to your account. That means... You're inside the building."

"I don't think so."

"Do you work here? Logged on for a sneak peek? If you stay out of the game 'til launch, I'll close my case out saying it was a glitch that I fixed. We don't have to make this more than it is."

"I've been retired for thirty-seven years, or more if the thing about the president you're giving me is right. I'm Jeremiah Harris. I was in the hospital. I uploaded and woke up here."

"That's not the name on the account you're signed into," he said. "If you won't be straight with me, then I'll have to boot you out and lock your account."

"You're not listening to me. Last thing I remember, I was dying in a hospital bed. I was supposed to go to Everafter."

"The digital retirement home? How did you end up here?"

"I was hoping you could tell me."

"What you're saying is impossible. You can't log into the system with an upload."

"I didn't log in. I woke up here. I don't know how I got here. I need help. Please, just reach out to Patty and she can verify everything."

"Okay... I'm going to have to look into it. I'll be in touch. Whatever you do, don't log out."

"Wait, are you going to reach out to Patty—Patricia Harris? Can you contact her for me? Let her know where I am?"

"Let me see what I can figure out. Assuming you're telling the truth, I'll get back to you."

"How long before I hear from you?" I asked.

"Umm... I'm not sure. Soon?"

"What am I supposed to do in the meantime?"

"Well, you could always play the game."

"Seriously?"

He shrugged. "You could just stand around if you want to. I'll get back to you as soon as I can, okay?"

Play the game. I was playing to find someone to get out of this mess and now that I have, he's telling me to keep playing.

"I don't know anything about this game. I'm terrible at it. I just want to leave."

"It's a fantasy military shooter based on the Saturn Moon Wars of the 3700s, with some liberties, of course." He typed on his tablet again. "There, I gave you the option to reset your character. Just follow the mission lines and try to have fun. I'll be in touch as soon as I can."

Have fun... If what he was telling me was true, years had passed since I was sitting in the hospital with Patty. It seemed like a few hours ago. How many years though?

Two... three? I was just at the hospital. I was in bad shape, but I remember sitting with Patty and then being wheeled out of the room. What had happened to Patty now? We were already in the winter of our lives, but she was holding up much better than I was. Was she still living in New Helsinki? Had she moved on? She probably thought I had died... *really* died. I couldn't blame her if she had. One step at a time. There was nothing I could do but wait and trust that Faizal would get back to me. I hoped he would be quick, but who knows how long he would take. Sitting around twiddling my thumbs wasn't an option. All I could do was keep playing this stupid game.

Chapter Six

My time spent in Paxor Seven wasn't going well so far. I was down a service drone and couldn't seem to handle the most basic enemies. Going back to a basement full of sarlocs didn't seem like the smartest thing to do. I needed to figure out why I was having so much trouble fighting them. The Weapons Boutique sounded like the place to go. I just didn't know where it was. I didn't have Buttons to show me the way either.

The NPCs couldn't help me contact Patty, but they should be able to help me in the game. There were several Marines standing around the city on guard duty. Maybe they could direct me to the Weapons Boutique.

I walked over to the two guards in front of headquarters. "Excuse me, could you tell me how to get to the Weapons Boutique?"

The guard raised a muscled arm and pointed over my left shoulder. "Southwest corner of the civilian district."

"Thanks," I said, turning to walk in the direction he had pointed.

I walked back into the civilian district, scanning rows of buildings until I found it. Inside, the walls were lined with all types of firearms. Stands of guns filled the middle of the room. A man was standing behind the counter. He was short and stocky, with spiked blond hair. As I approached, I realized it wasn't hair on his head but short quills. I didn't know what this thing was supposed to be, but it wasn't human.

"Welcome to the Weapons Boutique. I'm Silas. Here to pick out your service weapon?"

<Mission: Get Your Bearings>

<Mission Objective: Speak to Silas at the Weapons Boutique: Complete>

<Mission: Arm Yourself>

<Pick Out a Service Weapon from the Weapons Boutique>

<Reward: Service Weapon and Ammunition>

<Accept - Reject>

I accepted the mission and turned to Silas. "Nice to meet you, Silas. Yes, I'd love a new weapon. What are my options?"

"I've got everything from pistols to sniper rifles. For you..." He squinted at me in thought. "I'd recommend a pistol or maybe an SMG."

I paused. "What's the difference?"

"SMG, that's Sub-Machine Gun, is maneuverable and shoots fast. It uses pistol rounds, so the power isn't great, but what it lacks in power it makes up for with three-round burst and automatic fire. Of course, accuracy can be problematic. Spray and pray is the name of the game with an SMG. A pistol is easy to use and only takes one hand. It's not the best in any category but does well in all situations. It's hard to beat a good sidearm."

I already had a revolver that underwhelmed me. Picking up a second didn't sound like a good idea. I wanted something with more power. "What do you have with a little more punch?"

Silas grinned. "Well, if you want more stopping power, a tactical rifle or shotgun would do the trick. A shotgun is a close quarters weapon, but it's versatile. If you're using slugs, you can hit hard a little farther out, but you'll never have the range of a rifle. You can use specialized rounds for certain situations. A tactical rifle has longer range and higher capacity magazines. A shotgun is the best for sheer power. Which weapon you want depends on what tactics you use."

From what I've seen of this game so far, I would have to fight at close range. I liked the idea of the versatility of the shotgun, but a longer-range weapon would work for shorter range as well. I needed to figure out what kind of range we were talking about.

"What're the ranges of SMGs, shotguns, and tactical rifles?"

"SMGs and shotguns have a max range of forty meters, tactical rifles fifty. You can use accessories to increase the range if you need to reach out a little farther."

That didn't seem very different or accurate, but it was a game after all. Range didn't seem like a major factor.

"I'll try the shotgun," I said.

"You got it."

"How much are they?"

"The Federation covers your service weapon. If you wanted to contribute to start out with something a little nicer, that's certainly possible."

I pulled up my equipment to look at my credits.

"What can I get for 215 credits?" I asked.

Silas chuckled. "An accessory for your entry level shotgun and maybe some extra rounds. Got anything to sell or trade?"

I took out the armor pieces, revolver, and its ammunition and placed them on the table. The only thing left in my inventory was the Low Flow Injector and the envelope I'd forgotten all about. I took it out and opened it up.

<Mission: Mental Discipline>

<Report to the Psionic Training Institute to Begin Your Training as a Psionic Soldier>

<Class Unlock - Psionic>

<Accept - Reject>

A Psionic Soldier. It sounded cool, but also more involved than I wanted. I was only going to be around until Faizal could figure out that I was telling the truth and get me transferred to Everafter. All I wanted to do was shoot things and pass the time. I rejected the mission and tossed the letter onto the pile. It probably wasn't worth anything, but I wanted the best gun I could get.

"Does this change anything?"

When he picked up the paper, his eyes went wide. He looked up at me, then back down to the voucher. "Do you know what this is?"

"A voucher to get into the Psionic school."

"You don't want it? It's a prestigious school with limited attendance. People would kill to get their hands on this."

"I just want a nice gun. If that will get me one, I'm happy to trade it."

He grinned. "Let's have some fun then."

"Uh... All right."

He walked to a gun rack mounted to the wall behind the counter. He reached under the bottom of the rack and pressed a button. There was a loud click. The rack slid forward and then to the side, revealing a safe. He typed in a code and turned the handle, unlocking the massive metal box. He pulled it open and brought out two guns.

"With the voucher, I have two shotguns you can choose from. These weapons are top of the line. Not the junk the Federation uses. They're ten gauge and have a large selection of attachments. You can equip two attachments, so choose them well."

He placed the first one on the counter in front of me. A serious looking weapon. It was short and stubby. It didn't have a stock, just a hand grip.

"This is the Tsogov Slaughter-76. It shoots fast with excellent maneuverability. It's semiautomatic with a twelve-round magazine." He placed the other shotgun on the counter. This one looked long and sleek, with a tube running under the barrel almost as long as the barrel itself.

"This is the Winlite Instant Karma. It's also semi-automatic but instead of a detachable magazine it has a tube magazine under the barrel. That's a nice feature if you need to shoot a variety of different shells. The longer barrel gives it more punch and longer effective range. It can hold eight rounds in the tube with one in the chamber for a nine-round capacity."

"Wouldn't it be harder to reload the tube verses swapping out a magazine?" I asked.

"No, there are these tube-style loaders that can load five rounds at once. You can also load single rounds. The last round you put in will be the next to fire, so if you need a special round, you can put one in without unloading the gun or put in a string of five with the tube loader. With some practice, you'll never run out of rounds. Whatever you choose, I'll throw in some ammunition to get you started."

I held out a hand to the Instant Karma. "Can I take a look at this one?"

"Sure, try it on," Silas said. "See how it feels."

Since I was going to be playing solo until I actually made it to the retirement home, the Instant Karma seemed to make the most sense. The weapon with the most power would kill things the fastest... if I could hit them. Running out of ammo could end badly for me since the only help I had was from a service drone with no offensive capabilities. Silas said if I used it correctly, I would never run out. No more awkward reloads in the middle of combat. I picked up the shotgun and shouldered it. It felt good, well balanced and comfortable. Just what you would expect from such a fancy weapon.

"This looks good, I'll take this one."

<Equipping this item will bind it to you - Do you want to continue?>

<Yes - No>

I selected Yes.

<Mission Complete: Arm Yourself>

<Mission Rewards>

<100 Experience>

<Winlite Instant Karma>

<Slugs X 30>

<You have Reached Level Two>

Chapter Seven

Silas took the letter, put it back in the envelope, and slid it into an inside pocket in his jacket. "Pleasure doing business with you."

He didn't touch the rest of the junk on the counter.

I held a hand out to the pile. "What about all this?"

"Our bargain was for the letter," he said. "That's still yours."

I moved everything back into my inventory. I picked up a tube, lined it up, and used my thumb to slide the shotgun shells into the receiver. The tube pushed three in, leaving two in the tube.

"You still need to cock it and you can get one more in," Silas said.

I grabbed the handle, giving it a quick pull, and released it. The bolt slammed forward, chambering a slug with a satisfying *cha-chunk*.

I lined the tube up again when Silas stopped me. "Put the tube in your ammo pouch, then pull out the one round you need."

I wasn't sure how that was going to work, but he seemed to know what he was talking about. After dropping the tube with two rounds into my pouch, I stuck my hand in. I expected to just find the tube there, but to my surprise, I felt a single shell. I pulled it out and slid it into the receiver. It seemed I could pull ammo from the pouch as I wanted it. I turned the gun over in my hands, noticing a small screen built into the back of the rifle. It showed a nine with a red dot in the bottom left corner.

"Thanks," I said. "This display is the number of rounds in the shotgun?"

"Yes, sir, like I said, top of the line. You'll enjoy it."

"What's the red dot?" I asked.

"It's the auto-safety. It will turn on and off depending on if the area you're in is designated as a combat zone. Red means the safety is on, green for weapons hot."

I wasn't sure how I felt about a gun that turned itself off, but if I was in a safe zone, I shouldn't need it. It occurred to me that my pistol might have an auto safety as well, but I just didn't know it. I thanked him and put the items on the counter back into my bag before heading for the door.

Silas called after me. "If you need some accessories, come see me."

I gave him a wave as I left the shop. Those sarlocs had a surprise coming. Surely with a gun like this I would make quick work of them. I beelined for the Drone Warehouse. Cassandra was still standing outside when I made it back.

She looked confused when she saw me. "I thought you were in the basement."

"Working on it," I said, walking by without stopping.

The door to the basement was still open. I readied my shotgun and walked down the stairs. I moved to the right, ready to see what my new weapon could do. The sarloc I had killed was still lying on the floor with a faint glow. I moved up and nudged it with my foot.

<You have Received 3 Credits>

<You Can Loot the Following:>

<Corroded Metal Boots>

<Blue Tuber>

<Loot All - Abandon>

I selected Loot All and the body disintegrated. The boots I had just looted were probably heavy armor as well, judging from the name. I was right. Why did I keep getting armor I couldn't wear?

Even though I had killed one of them, two sarlocs were back in the corner. Must have respawned. I saw Buttons on the floor in a heap. It looked destroyed. Its multimeter in my HUD was grayed out. Even though all the bars were at zero, I thought I could fix it since the multimeter was still showing. That problem could wait. I aimed at one of the sarlocs and pulled the trigger. The shotgun bucked from the recoil, booming like a cannon. The slug slammed into the cabinet behind the sarlocs, punching a hole in it.

They started running at me from across the room. I fired, this time hitting the floor beside them. They made it halfway across the room by the time the shotgun's action cycled. This wasn't any better than the pistol. I ran up the stairs, stopping at the top to turn and aim. The sarlocs came to the bottom of the stairs, shuffled around, and then disappeared back into the basement. It was good to know they wouldn't follow me out.

I looked at my weapons.

<General Issue Revolver>

<Level: 1 - Common>

<Pistol>

<Damage: 16–26>

<Range: 40 Meters>

<Durability: 46/100>

<Winlite Instant Karma>

<Level: 1 - Legendary>

<Shotgun - Player Bound>
<Refinement Zero>
<Attachment 1: None>
<Attachment 2: None>
<Damage: 44–74>
<Range: 40 Meters>
<Durability: 250/250>
<Value: 10,000 Credits>

Ten thousand credits... That was a crazy number. The shotgun was good, but not that much better than the revolver. There must be more to it I wasn't aware of. It had a refinement characteristic the pistol didn't. Maybe that was why it was worth so much. Comparing the two weapons, I couldn't see why I would ever use the revolver. Not that either of them could hit anything. I headed for the Weapons Boutique. Silas had some explaining to do. My Instant Karma was better than my pistol by the numbers, but it didn't work.

"I'll be back," I said to Cassandra as I passed her standing outside her shop.

I walked down the street to the Weapons Boutique to find Silas behind the counter, twirling a revolver like a cowboy.

"Back so soon?" he asked. "Did you want to take a look at some of those accessories I was talking about?"

I placed my shotgun on the counter. "I'm actually having some trouble. I was getting attacked and couldn't hit anything with it. Do I need to sight it in or something?"

"There's nothing wrong with that gun," Silas said.

"Well, it doesn't shoot for shank," I said. "Shank... What the frag?"

I wasn't much of a curser, but here I couldn't curse at all. Instead, a different word came out of my mouth against my will.

"This is a civilized establishment. I'd appreciate it if you watch your language," he said, snatching the rifle off the counter and heading for the back of the shop. "Come on."

I followed him out the back door to a shooting range. There were ten stations with benches and corresponding targets. Silas didn't bother stepping up to the firing line. As soon as a target was in sight, he raised the gun and fired five shots in rapid succession. He walked to the control panel and pressed a button. The target started moving uprange toward us on a mechanical device. I walked over to him to see the results.

He turned around to face me and slammed the shotgun into my chest. "The problem with this rifle is about a foot behind the sight."

He walked back into the shop as the target approached. When it came to a stop, I found the center of the target was gone. There was a single jagged hole in the paper. The gun worked. There was no question about that. It had to be an issue with me... my character.

I pulled up my character sheet and scanned through the stats and skills. My class was listed as Engineer. There were five stats: Body, Grace, Intellect, Fortitude, and Psyche. I looked at the stat descriptions. Body increased melee damage and accuracy, added to energy, and damage reduction. Grace increased ranged damage and accuracy and added evasion. Intellect improved skills and Psionic damage and accuracy. Fortitude added hit points, resistances to natural effects, and added energy. Psyche buffed Psionic power and Psionic resistance. My most important stat seemed to be Grace. That was a problem because it was one of my lowest at eleven. My highest stats were intellect with a fifteen and psyche at thirteen.

Whoever built this character clearly intended to be a Psionic. Not surprising considering the invitation to the Psionic school. At the bottom of the sheet, I saw a back arrow. I touched it and got a popup.

<Would you like to reset your character? This can only be done once. Current allocations will be lost.>

<Yes - No>

I selected Yes. The character sheet cleared.

Chapter Eight

First, I had to select a name. Specter was still listed. I liked it. There was a poetic truth to it. I was a ghost in the game, after all. Next was species. I had four options. Human, Grolan, Tweld, and Axoroli. I selected each species, trying to figure out what the differences were.

<Human>

<After developing faster than light travel, Humans left Earth to explore the galaxy, discovering other sentient species along the way. They established the Federation to secure peaceful and lucrative interplanetary trade. Humans are versatile and resilient, gaining plus one to their primary stat every five levels and receiving a bonus to reputation.>

Humans seemed familiar enough. I could customize my avatar's appearance with any skin tone, hair, and eye color. I could also fine-tune my face and body to look any way

I wanted. Before moving on, I looked at what the other species were.

<Grolan>

<Tall humanoids from the distant jungle world Grolor. Grolan were the first species humans discovered after taking to the stars. Grolan and humans formed the Federation.>

Grolan were taller than humans with skin tones that ranged from green to purple. They had fair features and no hair. I found options for intricate tattoos that covered their bodies. They had bonuses to Grace and Fortitude with an agile movement ability that increased movement and climb speed.

<Tweld>

<The only thing hotter than the famed Tweld temper is their volcanic home world Draxol. After a short war with the Federation, Tweld kept their distance from the Federation for two centuries before becoming the third member.>

Tweld were shorter and stocky. I hadn't realized it until now, but Silas was a Tweld. They had short quills on their heads that ran down their backs. The skin that wasn't covered with quills looked tough, almost like rock. They had bonuses to body and fortitude with a thick skin ability that increased damage reduction and plasma resistance.

<Axoroli>

<The water world Lobritha is the home of the carnivorous Axoroli species. While Lobritha wasn't the last planet with intelligent life to be discovered, the Axorolis' strong connection to their home world made them the last species to join the Federation.>

Axoroli were roughly human-sized salamander people. I recognized it immediately as Colonel Radim's species. What I had thought was hair turned out to be gills on the side of their heads that draped down their backs. Their skin could be any color with separate color choices for the gills. They had bonuses to psyche and intellect with a water-breathing ability and low-light vision.

I still knew nothing about character creation. Humans or Grolan seemed like good choices for an engineer, but I suspected that any of the species could be good at anything. If I were going to be playing the game for real, I would probably stick with human. How often do you get to be a different species, though? I was curious. It might be fun to do something new. I selected Grolan.

I had customization options with skin color and tattoos. After a few minutes of looking, I settled on a light blue skin tone without any tattoos. Next was the option to select a primary and secondary attribute. I knew Grace was my most important stat, so I selected it first. I wasn't sure about a secondary stat. Body looked promising for damage reduction, which could be nice, or Fortitude for some extra hit points. I didn't know what effect intellect would have. Psyche would protect against Psionic attacks, but that sounded like something I would run into later on in the game, so I probably wouldn't ever need it. I settled on Fortitude for the extra hit points.

Next was class selection. I scanned through the six options and their descriptions.

<Heavy Trooper: Armored front-line troops specialized in close combat. Unlocks the ability to use mechanized battle suits. Roles: Tank/DPS>

<Grunt: Weapons specialists deadly at any range. Roles: Tank/DPS>

<Combat Medic: Uses nanobots to heal and inflict damage and afflictions. Roles: Healer/DPS>

<Engineer: Experts with technological systems. Uses drones to augment abilities of the player and party. Roles: DPS/Healer>

<Force Recon: Operates behind enemy lines to gather intelligence and conduct covert operations. Specialist using stealth and subterfuge. Roles: DPS>

<Psionic: Unlockable through the store. Wide range of mental powers used for offense and defense. Roles: DPS>

I didn't want to start over completely, so I stuck with engineer.

Skills were next. I had two skill slots free to customize my character, but I didn't know what that meant. I clicked on the information tab in the skill bar.

<Skills determine what your character can do in the game. Your character starts with preassigned class skills and two skill slots for customization. After character creation, you can learn new skills through training by a qualified professional. You can learn an unlimited number of skills. There are five skill tiers that can be leveled up through use. Attempting to use a skill you aren't proficient in results in an automatic failure.>

I started by checking the basics for my class. In the skills tab, I found my weapon skills. I had pistols, sub-machine guns, and tactical rifles. I noticed shotguns weren't on the list. That explained why I couldn't hit anything in the basement. They all showed zero except pistol, which had a skill of four.

Skills related to my class were light and medium armor, engineering, and drone repair. I also had medicine. Two skill slots were available to select additional skills. I found shotgun in the weapons list and selected it for my first slot. Looking at the engineering section, I found some possibilities: Fabrication, Improvised Mechanics, and Scavenging.

Scavenging was straightforward, finding useful parts off of broken machinery. Fabrication let me design and build drone systems. Improvised Mechanics would let me substitute items and parts when I didn't have what I needed, but reduced the quality of the end product. I didn't know what to pick. Scavenging might be the biggest payoff in the limited time I would be here, so I selected it.

From Silas' shooting display, and the fact that my shotgun skill was zero, I knew I wanted to level my skill up before I tried to fight the sarlocs again. I reloaded the shotgun and went to an empty range. After I fired all nine rounds, I checked my shotgun skill.

<Shotgun: 8>

I reloaded and fired another nine before checking my skill again.

<Shotgun: 10>

That second round hadn't paid off as much as the first. A skill cap could explain the diminishing rewards, if there was one. I checked the two targets I had used. I'd been hitting the target. The first one was a little all over the place, but the second had a much nicer grouping. Not as nice as Silas' shooting, but I was hitting the target. I didn't want to use all my rounds and have to buy more if I wasn't going to get any skill for it. This was as good as it was going to get. I could always run up the stairs if the sarlocs were still trouble.

I went back in the shop. Silas was still playing with the pistol. He gave me the side-eye as I walked over to the counter.

"Two tubes for the shotgun please," I said.

He jabbed the pistol in my direction to accentuate his point as he spoke. "Don't come into my shop accusing me of selling shoddy goods."

"You're right. It's a great shotgun. I was blaming the gun when the shortcoming was my own. I apologize."

His expression softened. "Well, all right then." He took two tubes from under the counter. "Two tubes, and the range fee, comes to forty credits."

Forty credits. I'd seen notifications about receiving credits but had no idea how to produce them to buy something. I opened my inventory. At the bottom of the screen, it showed my currency. There was a picture of a circular emblem with a zero beside it and FC215.

"FC... That's Federation credits?"

Silas had a quizzical look. "Yes, of course."

"Of course... forty Federation credits coming up," I said and then mumbled, "as soon as I figure out how to do it."

Forty credits, I thought, staring at the total. A credstick materialized in my hand. The total displayed dropped to

175. I handed it to him and picked up the tubes, reloaded the shotgun, and dropped the extra shell into my ammo pouch. I gave Silas a salute before turning and leaving.

Chapter Nine

Third time's a charm, at least I hoped it was. I found my way back to the Drone Warehouse feeling hopeful but nervous about how my next try with the sarlocs would go.

Cassandra shot me a smirk as I walked inside. "Having trouble?"

"I'm working on it!" I shouted as I crossed the shop and stomped down the stairs.

The red safety on the shotgun switched to green when I reached the bottom. The two sarlocs were back in their spot on the far side of the room.

"If this doesn't work, I'm going to find a bar."

I aimed and squeezed the trigger. The shell slammed into the sarloc, knocking it back into the cabinet. The second one turned and charged. I fired again, dropping it as well. It was such a drastic difference from the pistol I couldn't believe it. One shot kills and my accuracy issues seemed to be resolved.

"This is more like it," I said.

I walked over to the glowing spot in the corner, placed another trap, and armed it.

<Mission: Pest Control>

<Objective: Set Sarloc Traps 2/4>

When I stood up, I saw a crate right in front of my face. I opened it.

<You Can Loot the Following:>

I selected Loot All without looking at the contents.

<Mission: Pest Control>

<Bonus Objective: Low Flow Injectors 2/4>

I found another crate on the way to the third circle and looted it.

<Mission: Pest Control>

<Bonus Objective: Low Flow Injectors 3/4>

I moved to the other side of the room, keeping an eye out for sarlocs. It was all clear, leaving me free to place and arm the next trap.

<Mission: Pest Control>

<Objective: Set Sarloc Traps 3/4>

On my way to set the last trap, I spotted a sarloc on top of one of the shelves in the middle of the room. It was standing on a crate.

I raised my rifle. "Sneaky fragger."

I pulled the trigger. It fell lifeless off the shelf and hit the floor. I couldn't reach the crate from the floor. I had to stand on the bottom shelf to loot the crate.

<Mission: Pest Control>

<Bonus Objective: Low Flow Injectors: Complete>

I walked over to the last circle and armed the trap.

<Mission: Pest Control>

<Objective: Set Sarloc Traps: Complete>

This was more like it. I headed for the door before I remembered I had sarlocs to loot and a busted service drone on the floor. Maybe I would get something I could use instead of more heavy armor.

Looting the sarlocs was the next thing to do. I didn't take the time to look at what they had. I just selected Loot All as soon as the option popped up. There would be time to sort it out later. When I had finished, I picked up my battered service drone, went upstairs, and closed the hatch in the floor.

I had a couple of takeaways from my time in the basement. First, the Instant Karma was working well after I fixed my character. Second, Buttons was mostly useless. Yes, it could help me find places on the map, but that seemed lackluster. I was sure Cassandra could help me figure out what it could do. Buttons would need to be repaired and maybe I could get it some upgrades. Anything to add a little utility would be great. There had to be more to it and I needed to figure out what. Lastly, I wanted to look at the game settings. The constant messages and loot boxes were already getting annoying. There had to be something I could do to streamline the play a little.

I found Cassandra standing outside the shop.

"How'd it go?" she asked.

"I did it. The traps are set, and I killed all the sarlocs I could find."

"And the low flow injectors?"

"Oh, I have them right here."

I opened my inventory and took out the injectors.

"That's fantastic! I guess I owe you some credits," she said, reaching into her pocket.

She pulled out a credstick and traded it for the injectors.

<Mission: Pest Control: Complete>

<Mission Rewards>

<150 Experience>

<Bonus Objective: 150 Experience>

<50 Reputation: Port Bax Shopkeepers Union>

<25 Credits>

<You have Reached Level Three>

Cassandra looked at the drone in my arms. "I'm sorry your friend had so much trouble. It'll need some work to get back to full operation."

"How would I do that exactly?"

"You studied drone repair in basic, right?"

I shrugged. "Let's assume I slept through basic."

"I'll give you a refresher, then. You'll need some parts and some tools. Luckily, I have them for sale in my shop. Come on in. We'll get you sorted out."

I followed her inside. She went around the shop to a bin with mechanical components and pulled some out. She walked over and put them on the counter. It looked like pieces of robots, nothing that would go with my drone.

"All right the last thing you need is a beginning repair tool. This should do the trick," she said, reaching under the counter.

She brought up a large wrench. I didn't see any bolts on the drone, so I wasn't sure how I was going to fix a smashed-up drone with a wrench, but she seemed to know her stuff.

"A spanner and two repair parts. How does seventy credits sound?"

I ran a hand over my chin. "I mean... fifty sounds better."

"Don't get me wrong, I like you, but I don't like you that much. It's seventy. Take it or leave it."

"I'll take," I said, producing the credits.

"Pleasure doing business with you," she said.

I looked at the counter. A busted-up drone, some spare pieces, and a wrench. "Okay, how do I do this?"

"Just pick up the repair parts and use the spanner to fix the drone."

I moved the repair parts into my inventory. I'd picked up a lot of items from my time in the basement. The parts took up the last open slot in my backpack. I picked up the spanner and looked at the destroyed drone, wondering what I was supposed to do. Did I have to take it apart? Check the wiring? How could I do any of that with a wrench?

"I don't see how I'm supposed to fix this."

Cassandra gave me a pitiful look. "Just touch the spanner to the drone."

I tapped the spanner to the top of Buttons' dome. When it made contact, the drone's health started going up.

<Repair Part has been consumed.>

The repair parts were slowly being used as the drone's health went up. When all three had been consumed the drone's health was full. The drone stood up on the counter, looking good as new. This meant skills were passive. I didn't have to know anything about what I was doing for real. I just needed the right tools and materials.

Cassandra looked at my uniform. "Those sarlocs did a number on you. You look like you were dragged behind a rhino. Don't let the Colonel see you like that."

"I don't want to spend on a new uniform right now," I said. "It'll have to last for a while."

"You don't need a new uniform, just head over to the readiness center and jump in the GRM. That stands for gear repair module, in case you had forgotten that too."

"Oh yeah, the good ole GRM, of course I know it," I lied. "Before I head over there, my backpack is getting full. Is there somewhere I can sell things I don't want? What do I do with this stuff?"

"You can sell at any shop. You can deal with a shopkeeper directly or just use the interfaces," she said, holding a hand out to a computer on the end of the counter. "It doesn't really make a difference since prices are set by the Federation. There is a little wiggle room but you can't expect to get deals unless they like you."

"How do I make them like me?"

"Build relationships. Do jobs for them to lay the groundwork and after you've gained their trust, you can officially represent an organization by wearing its insignia. Your heroic deeds will bring honor to the organization and raise your standing with them."

I stepped up to the interface. There were three tabs: Buy, Sell, and Buy Back. I selected Sell and a list of items from my inventory appeared on the screen. I could select individual items or sell all items of a specific quality level at once. Since I didn't know what I had, I didn't want to do that. I scrolled through the list of items. I knew I couldn't use any of the heavy armor I'd gotten, so I selected those first. There were a lot of things I didn't know what they were for. I had a couple blue tubers, a cracked gear, and potent bark, among other things. As I scrolled through the list, I found a piece of light armor, Frayed Webbing.

I didn't know if it was any good, but it was armor I could wear. I also found a weapon called a drone bomb thrower I could sell for twenty-five credits. Maybe I could put that on my service drone and get some help in combat? Corroded armor plating didn't sound like it would be useful going forward. I selected everything except my spanner, the frayed webbing, and the drone bomb thrower. I hit the sell button.

<You have Received 135 Credits>

"Thanks, Cassandra," I said, heading for the door. "Talk to you later."

I headed out of the shop, taking a left outside. I'd made it twenty paces, with Buttons in tow, before Cassandra called after me. "Hey, Specter."

I turned around.

"The readiness center is that way," she said, pointing in the opposite direction.

I spun on my heel, heading in the other direction. As I passed her, I said, "Some people don't appreciate the scenic route, I guess."

Chapter Ten

I had seen the Readiness Center in the military district earlier. It was close to headquarters, if I remembered correctly. I could ask Buttons, but I decided to just see if I was getting familiar with the city. If the drone was destroyed again I'd have to get around on my own. I started walking toward HQ.

"Have a sec?" a voice said from behind me.

I turned around to see Faizal standing in the street. "I've got nothing but time. What did you find out?"

"I don't have a resolution for you yet, but I've been looking into your situation, and I wanted to give you an update."

"That's great! What's the good news?"

"Well... Do you want to find somewhere to sit down? This might come as a shock."

My stomach churned. It surprised me to have such a physical reaction. "What is it?"

"We looked you up. I don't know how to tell you this but... you're dead."

"I know I'm dead," I said. "Hello? Trapped in a game here!"

"No, I mean, you've been declared legally dead. Consciousness lost. As far as the world knows, your upload either didn't work or there was some kind of problem. I don't know the details yet. I've put in a request for your file to the authorities, but haven't gotten a response yet."

I nodded slowly, letting it sink in. "Okay, that's inconvenient, but we can just call Patty and she'll get it all worked out. Were you able to find her?"

He looked down at his tablet. I got the impression he was stalling.

"What? What is it?"

Faizal sighed. "That was nine years ago."

"What was?"

"When you were declared dead."

"Nine years? How is that possible?"

"I'm still working on that."

I did the math in my head. "But that means it's... 5354?"

"Actually it's 5355."

I was afraid I knew the answer to my next question. "What about Patty?"

"She passed a few years ago. I'm sorry."

"It's okay," I said. "We'll just have to contact Patty at Everafter and once I'm transferred, I'll make it up to her."

"No, I mean… she didn't upload. She's gone," he said. "I called Everafter to make sure. They said she hadn't uploaded, and her contract was canceled four years ago."

"Oh," I said. My heart dropped into my stomach. "Are you sure? I mean, how do you know you have the right person?"

He tapped on his tablet. "Patty Harris. A teacher from New Helsinki. Born October 30th, 5240… died May 14th, 5352."

"She's not dead," I said. "You need to keep looking."

I didn't know how I knew it, but I did. She was still out there somewhere.

Faizal sighed. "I don't know what to tell you. We're still looking into your situation. I'll let you know when we find out more."

"Thanks. I appreciate you letting me know."

"No problem… I'll be in touch."

"Hold on a sec before you go," I said. "I want to change some game settings to streamline play a little. How would I do that?"

"You can find the settings menu in your character sheet. Look for a gear icon in the bottom right corner."

"Thanks," I said. "I appreciate your help."

"I'll let you know more as soon as I can," he said before disappearing.

Patty couldn't be gone... she just couldn't. Neither one of us thought we had *forever*, but we should've had longer than this. I just had a hard time believing it. Did she think I had died and decided not to upload because of it? That didn't sound like something she would do. She spent the last nine years without me though, so who knows what had happened or how she was feeling. I wish I could talk to her... No. I would feel it if she were gone. She was out there somewhere.

My thoughts shifted to what that meant for me. We had friends, but most of them were our age. Helping me would be a huge hassle. I'd have to have my death reversed. That would take legal proceedings, which meant time and money. Not that I had a way to contact anyone to ask in the first place. That was all assuming they were still alive. I wasn't aware of any cases like mine. There's no telling how hard it would be. If Patty was gone, that meant our life savings were gone, too. I was at the mercy of whoever ran the game. I had no money or way to contact anyone to get my life back. Worrying wasn't going to help anything. All I could do was stay busy until Faizal got back to me. He would sort out the mix-up and find Patty. I just needed to hold on until he did.

The Readiness Center sat opposite the Medical Center. I stopped before going inside, wanting to check my settings before I forgot. The settings menu was right where Faizal said it would be. I scanned through the options, noticing a few sections I wanted to investigate further.

Parental controls were first. Language filters and graphic content were both turned on. Language filters would filter player and NPC dialog for offensive language. That explained why I couldn't curse and the game was auto-replacing me. I took a look at the graphic content filter. Disabling the filter would show blood and gore. I wasn't sure how graphic it would be, but I didn't feel like finding out. Considering how real the rest of the game felt I expected it would be *graphic*. The blue pixelated effects were good enough for me.

After a few minutes of digging around, I found loot settings and located the options for Auto Loot.

<Turning on Auto Loot will loot all available items without prompting you until your inventory is full. Looted items can be reviewed in the game log.>

Sounded perfect. I enabled it. Auto Loot could be refined to not loot items of certain qualities based on the six levels: junk, common, uncommon, rare, epic, and legendary. I didn't put a restriction on it. Lastly, I found a section for notifications and changed the mission notifications to only show when picking up or completing a mission. That should reduce all the notifications. I wanted to minimize distractions as much as I could. There was just too much going on.

With my settings reviewed, it was time to change gears and look at my inventory. I needed to look at the frayed belt. I selected it and the belt I was wearing to compare.

<Basic Webbing>

<Slot: Waist>

<Value: 1 Credit>

<Frayed Webbing>

<Level: 1 - Junk>

<Light Armor - Bind on Equipment>

<Quickdraw 1>

<Armor: 2>

<Slot: Waist>

<Durability: 25/25>

<Value: 12 Credits>

I didn't know what a quick draw slot was, but the new belt was actually armor, even if it was paltry. I equipped the frayed webbing. The basic webbing I was wearing disintegrated into blue pixels and the frayed webbing appeared in its place. It had a single strap running across my chest from the lower right to top left. There was a circular disc in middle. It reminded me of the magtech system I used in the military. I pulled up my equipment and noticed I had a new slot available. It was listed as Quickdraw 1.

It looked like a normal equipment slot. I took my spanner and moved it into the quickdraw slot. It appeared on my chest, attached to the disc. I grabbed the spanner and pulled it off. It came away freely. When I touched it to the spot on the strap again, it clicked into place as if a magnet held it. So, the quickdraw let me access an item without having to pull it out of my inventory. That could be handy. I checked my inventory. The spanner wasn't in my backpack, freeing up a slot.

With that sorted, I stepped into the Readiness Center. I'd expected to see someone sitting behind a desk or standing behind a counter. There wasn't anyone inside. I found large clear tubes, similar to what I'd seen in the Medical Center. They had an opening in the front large enough to step inside. I went to the closest tube and found a control panel outside consisting of a screen and a single green button.

I pressed the button. A panel opened in the top of the tube. A cone-shaped light ran over me. After the scan was complete, a popup appeared.

<Repair All Items 37 Credits>

<Continue - Abort>

I selected Continue. Lights in the tube's floor lit up and I stepped inside. The tube flashed a bright light that made it impossible to see for just a second and then faded away. I looked down to see my uniform appeared brand new. Between the fees to repair my equipment and the medical center, it had taken me almost fifty credits to recover from my death. I definitely couldn't afford to keep dying.

I stepped out of the tube where Buttons was waiting. "That was easy."

Buttons wiggled its camera in response. I pulled up my mission log to check my progress.

<Mission: Get Your Bearings>

<Familiarize Yourself with Port Bax>

<Mission Objectives:>

<Speak to Cassandra at the Drone Warehouse: Complete>

<Speak to Silas at the Weapons Boutique: Complete>

<Speak to Boris at the Armor Emporium>

<Speak to Doctor Silvers at the Medical Treatment Center: Complete>

<Speak to Parson at the Enlisted Club>

I still had another mission I hadn't started yet.

<Mission: Settling In>

<Locate Your Locker in the Barracks>

I thought I knew where the barracks were. Those four buildings with insignias hanging on the front of them. I hadn't found the Armor Emporium yet. Completing the barracks should be easy. I walked back to where I had come out of the hangar and found the four buildings with brigade insignias. I walked over to the one with the eleven insignia and went in.

Inside, there were four large round tables with chairs. Rows of bunks with lockers at the foot of each filled up the rest of the rectangular building. There were plenty of lockers, I just had to find mine. I walked over to the first one. It had a digital panel on the front. I tried to open it.

<To use locker storage, you must register a unique eight-digit passcode.>

<Would you like to proceed?>

<Register - Abort>

I selected Register and entered my birthday, 03245242.

<Registration: Complete>

The screen changed to a login. I entered my code and the door opened.

<Mission Complete: Settling In>

<Rewards: 25 Experience>

I opened the door. It was just a locker. I supposed it worked like a real locker and I could store items in it. I pulled up my equipment and had a new tab labeled

Locker. It had ten slots available. I wanted to test it out. I needed something to put in it. The only things in my backpack were basic webbing, and the drone bomb thrower. I transferred both over in the menu. They materialized inside. I took the revolver off my belt and placed it in the locker as well. It appeared on my locker inventory. I could add items through my inventory or manually. It locked automatically when I closed the door.

Chapter Eleven

Pour Decisions was in the middle of the courtyard with two barracks on either side. Since it was so close, it made sense to tackle that one next. I walked into a military-themed bar. The walls were full of guns and equipment used as decorations. Guidons with the symbol of the Federation Marines—the shield with orbiting planets—hung over the bar with two brigade banners on either side. The bar was on the far wall with round tables and chairs taking up most of the middle of the room. On the right side were vintage games from the distant past. I knew of the games, but didn't know how to play. There were tables lined with green felt, circular boards split into sections with numbers around the outside, as well as a green table with a small net in the middle.

"Hey there, Marine, welcome to Pour Decisions. What can I get ya?"

I hadn't noticed the person behind the counter. It was an Axoroli. He stood about six feet tall with charcoal skin that lightened under his neck. Wide shoulders and large muscles threatened to burst out of a beige button-up shirt with the sleeves rolled up to his elbows. He had a large scar running from his elbow to his wrist that was deep enough to deform his arm. His gills were a deep purple and hung down to his shoulders.

I walked over to the bar and sat down. "Just looking around."

"There're really three things you can find in Pour Decisions, besides good company. Food, drink, and the bounty board," he said, pointing at a billboard mounted to the wall. "If you need some work, I have a job you could do."

"What do you need?"

"First things first," he said, extending a webbed hand. "I'm Parson. Proprietor of Pour Decisions."

I shook his webbed hand. "Specter."

<Mission: Get Your Bearings>

<Speak to Parson at the Enlisted Club: Complete>

"You should never discuss business on an empty stomach. Let me get you a menu," he said.

"Do we have business to discuss?" I asked.

"Eat first, then we'll talk."

He produced a single laminated page. I hadn't realized I was hungry until I looked at the menu. It was strange being hungry in a game. One thing they told me about Everafter was that they eliminated hunger. People there just ate for pleasure without the worry of unwanted weight gain. The menu was split into breakfast, lunch, and dinner with a note that everything was available 24/7. I had always been a fan of breakfast, but since I got sick, I'd been on a restrictive diet. Since I didn't have a body anymore, that shouldn't be a problem. That was assuming food here actually tasted like anything. I looked over the menu.

"Let me have chocolate chip pancakes with a side of sausage," I said.

"And to drink?"

"Dealer's choice."

"Sidewinder it is," he said.

He filled a glass with a dark beer and placed it on the counter in front of me. I took a sip. It tasted like... beer, not cheap beer either, the good craft stuff I used to get. The beer was a little sweet and a little bitter, with a velvety texture. My pancakes arrived after a few minutes with some maple syrup. I poured a heavy dose of syrup and took a bite. Sweet, chocolaty goodness filled my mouth. The Sidewinder went well with the chocolate in the pancakes.

I gulped them both down. When I had finished, I noticed a new icon beside my map with a sixty-minute timer.

<Well Fed: +10% Health and Energy>

Parson came over and leaned against the counter. "How was it?"

"Delicious. Pancakes were fantastic and that beer really hit the spot."

"Down to business then. I'd like to get my hands on some of the local flora and fauna to see what I can make with it. If you can collect some for me, I'd be happy to pay you for your trouble."

<Mission: Local Flavors>

<Collect Ten Cooking Ingredients.>

<Rewards: 250 Experience, 50 Credits, C Ration>

<Accept - Reject>

I accepted the mission. "Happy to help. I'll take the check for now, though."

"Don't worry about that. The first meal's always free at Pour Decisions. My way of welcoming Marines to the planet."

"I appreciate that," I said. "Where'd you learn to cook like that?"

"Before I came to Paxor Seven, I was a culinary specialist on board the *Excalibur*. It's a galactic destroyer. By the end of my third tour, I was running the mess hall. I wanted a change of pace, so I requested a position here near the front lines. Are you interested in cooking?"

"If I can make stuff like those pancakes, then yeah. How would I get into it?"

"I have a recipe book I've put together that can get you started. It's fifty credits. I'll even throw in a camp stove. If you need ingredients, I can sell them to you from the restaurant's stores."

I knew I could have an unlimited number of skills, so why not give cooking a shot?

I produced a credstick with the fifty credits and slid it across the bar. "Sure, I'll take it."

Parson pulled a stout book and a small gas camp stove out from behind the bar and handed them to me. I put the camp stove in my inventory. The cover of the book said *Parson's Introduction to Cooking*. I opened the book.

<Would you like to learn Beginning Cooking?>

<Accept - Reject>

I accepted. The book disappeared into blue pixels.

<You have learned Beginning Cooking. Skills can be viewed in the skills tab of your character sheet.>

I opened my character sheet, finding the cooking skill added with a skill of one out of one hundred. Focusing on the skill made a separate popup appear for the cooking skill. I had three recipes listed: Burnt kabobs, charred vegetables, and crispy rolls. I selected the burnt kabobs.

<Burnt Kabobs>

<Ingredients: Hunk of Meat>

<Eating Burnt Kabobs will restore 30 Hunger.>

I remembered that I had gotten a bunch of things that could have been cooking ingredients in the basement of the Drone Warehouse. Unfortunately, I'd sold them. When I first looked at the terminal in the Drone Warehouse, there was a buyback tab. I might be able to recover some of those items and make quick work of this mission. A terminal was mounted to the far side of the bar. I pulled up the menu and selected the buyback tab. The tab had fifteen slots. I scrolled through the items I'd sold and found some items that were used for cooking: Hunk of Meat, two Blue Tubers, and two Potent Bark. I bought them back for twelve credits and switched over to the buy tab to have a look. There were rows of ingredients listed, as well as completed dishes. I didn't want to spend my money buying ingredients. Equipment was more important. I would have to loot them from the mobs I killed.

I needed five more cooking ingredients to complete the quest, or I could use them to work on my cooking skill. Hanging onto them made more sense. Maybe I could find some more sarlocs lurking around to finish the mission off. I got up and went to the bounty board. There were a few scraps of paper of different sizes and colors posted. I touched one.

<Mission: Special Delivery>

<The receiving office has a backlog of mail from off-world. Report to Private Barr to assist with the delivery of the mail backlog.>

<Rewards: 150 Experience, 30 Credits>

<Accept - Reject>

I accepted and tried another listing.

<Bounty Mission: Ambush Hunter>

<Patrols in the vicinity of Port Bax are being ambushed by an unknown creature. Intelligence reports that the creature only attacks at night using ambush tactics. Find the Ambush Hunter outside Port Bax at night and eliminate it. The first player to defeat the Ambush Hunter, and bring proof to Lieutenant Nash, will receive payment for completing the bounty.>

<Rewards: 500 XP, 200 Reputation: Federation Command, 250 Credits, 1 Medal>

<Accept - Reject>

I accepted this one too and went back to the board.

<Mission: Civil Discourse>

<A civilian crew is conducting illegal mining operations in the hills north of Port Bax. Locate the crew and shut down their operation.>

<Rewards: 250 Experience, 50 Credits, 125 Reputation: Federation Marines>

<Accept - Reject>

It was strange that the level four mission gave better rewards than a level six. It would make sense if the rewards only went to one person who completed it. There would be a lot of competition for a mission like that, if there were any other players. I accepted Civil Discourse. It was the last quest available from the board.

Chapter Twelve

The last piece of Get Your Bearings was to speak to Boris at the Armor Emporium. Since I was so close, it made sense to finish it before starting a new mission.

I asked Buttons, "Can you mark the Armor Emporium on the map, please?"

A green dot appeared on the edge of the map. I followed the dot, finding the emporium tucked away in the southeast corner of the civilian district. Inside the shop, I found rows of gear. Hats to boots and everything in between. A burly man with a thick black beard and a bald head stood behind the counter.

"Welcome to Armor Emporium!" he said in an accent that sounded like it came from Enceladus, a moon of Saturn covered in ice. "I am Boris Tsogov."

"Nice to meet you, Boris, I'm Jere... uh, Specter."

"I have the finest armor Federation has to offer. Feel free to look."

"Thanks," I said.

<Mission Complete: Get Your Bearings>

<Mission Reward: 600 Experience, 100 Reputation: Federation Marines>

A vest caught my attention. It was sleek and black, with armor plating woven onto the surface. I walked over to get a closer look.

"Good eye, comrade," Boris said. "Nightmare Battlegear, top of line protection against ballistic and energy weapons. Comes as set with added benefits."

It had a price tag hanging from it. I took a look, three thousand credits. I shook my head.

"What?" Boris asked. "You don't like?"

"A little light in the pocket, if you get my meaning," I said.

"I have job you could help with, I'll even throw in armor. Not Nightmare, but good."

"What do you need me to do?"

"There was package that came in on ship but was not delivered. Go pick up package and bring to me."

"Easy enough," I said. "Do you have a tracking number or something?"

"No tracking. Just go to spaceport, tell them Boris send you."

<Mission: Special Delivery>

<Retrieve the delivery from the spaceport and return it to the Armor Emporium.>

<Rewards: 200 Experience, Chest Armor>

<Accept - Reject>

I crossed town back into the military district where I had arrived on the ship. Sergeant Hopkins was still standing by the gate to the hangar.

He stepped in front of me as I tried to pass through. "Sorry, pacifist, no ships heading off planet today."

"I need to pick up a delivery for the Armor Emporium. Where would I do that?"

"Anything to stay out of the fight, I guess," he scoffed. "You need to talk to the receiving office."

"And... where might I find the receiving office?"

He pointed to a building in the middle of the spaceport. "It's the building that says Receiving Office."

"Thanks, Sergeant," I said.

I stepped around him and walked over to the building. In the front of the shop was a large counter with a metal door on rollers pulled down. It looked closed. I found a side door and knocked. After a minute, a woman answered. She had on a gray jumpsuit with grease smeared on it, as well as on her hands and face. The name and rank on her jumpsuit told me she was Private Barr.

"Where have you been?" she asked. "I've been waiting on you for over an hour now."

"I think you have me confused with someone else. I'm here to pick up a delivery for Boris at the Armor Emporium."

She looked defeated. "Oh, I thought you were the mechanic. Look, the delivery drone's broken. I've been trying to fix it, but it's beyond me. Tell Boris as soon as headquarters sends someone over to fix it, I'll get his shipment to him."

"Could I just take it? Get a delivery off your list?"

"Come on in," she said, stepping aside and holding the door open.

There was a large drone in the middle of the room. It stood twelve feet tall, painted yellow with metal pincers for hands and treads instead of legs. Rotating yellow lights were mounted to each shoulder. They were off. The building was full of crates stacked along the walls. It looked like the delivery drone had been offline for a while.

Private Barr walked over to one of the crates and leaned against it. "This is Boris's shipment. Unless you brought a cargo drone with you, you'll have to wait until my drone's fixed."

The crate was a five-foot cube, definitely not something I could move without help. I didn't want to wait around for a mechanic, assuming one was even coming.

"If you want to help, you could go see what's taking the mechanic so long or if you know anything about drone repair, you could take a look yourself."

<Objective Added: Special Delivery>

<Find a mechanic or repair the cargo drone, then escort the delivery back to the Armor Emporium with Boris's delivery.>

"Mind if I take a look at the drone?"

Private Barr sat on a stool by the counter. "Go for it."

I pulled out my wrench and touched it to the drone.

<Missing Components: Repair Parts>

"I need some repair parts," I said. "Let me get some at the Drone Warehouse and I'll get it going."

"There are some in the box beside the drone," she said. "I don't know if it'll be enough. This hunk-o-junk should have been scrapped years ago, if you ask me."

I found an open box on the floor beside the drone with repair parts inside. I added five of them to my inventory and tried again. This time I got a progress bar. It took noticeably longer to fill than when I repaired my service drone. When the bar was full the caution lights turned on and started spinning. The drone shuddered and straightened up.

"You did it! I'll get Boris's delivery out right now," Private Barr said. "This thing's always breaking down. Could you follow it over and make sure there's no trouble?"

"Happy to," I said.

She typed on a computer on the counter. A garage door on the side of the shop slid open as the drone rolled over to Boris's crate and picked it up. I followed it through the door and out of the hangar. We'd just crossed into the civilian district when sparks shot of the drone and it shuddered to a stop. I still had two repair parts from the Receiving Office. I touched my wrench to it again and got another progress bar. After one part was consumed, it sprang to life. It started moving again, rolling along with a strained shudder. It looked like it would break down any second, but we managed to make it to the Armor Emporium without another incident. Boris was waiting outside.

The drone placed the crate beside the door. A panel on the front of the drone opened, revealing a display that read, "Signature required."

Boris walked up to the touchscreen and squiggled his finger across it. The drone turned and shambled its way back to the spaceport.

<Mission Complete: Special Delivery>

<Rewards: 200 Experience, Chest Armor>

<Bonus Objective: 50 XP>

<You have Reached Level Four>

"Deal is deal. Come pick out armor," Boris said, going back in the shop. "What type do you want? Light, Medium, or Heavy?"

I knew I had skills for light and medium armor. Out of those two, medium seemed like it would offer the most protection. I also hadn't found any of it yet.

"Medium," I said.

Boris walked over to a piece of armor hanging on the wall, picked it up, and handed it to me. "Is good, *da*?"

I took the armor and inspected it.

<Basic Brigandine Vest>

<Required Level: 4 - Common>

<Medium Armor - Bind on Pick Up>

<Armor: 44>

<Slot: Chest>

<Durability: 85/85>

<Value: 35 Credits>

"Yes, it's good."

I equipped the vest and opened my character sheet. My armor was up to fifty-nine. I had 150 hit points and 143 energy.

"Thanks, Boris. This is going to help a lot. Duty calls. I'll catch up to you later."

I noticed a message icon beside my hit points. With a little trial and error, I figured out how to open the message.

<From: Lieutenant Nash>

<Message: I need you for an urgent mission. Report to headquarters for orders.>

I was about as far away from headquarters as I could get and still be in Port Bax. I wanted to collect all the missions I could get before I got started on them. My next stop was headquarters. It took me a few minutes to walk over. Inside, I found the same Marine sitting behind the desk in the lobby.

I stepped up to the desk. "Specter for Lieutenant Nash."

"He's expecting you. Down the hall, second door on the right."

I found the door open. Inside, a man with a scar running across his left eye sat behind a desk. I was suddenly unsure if I was expected to act in a certain way around officers. Should I salute? Knock? What exactly was the decorum that was expected? Erring on the side of politeness, I stepped into the doorway and knocked.

Lieutenant Nash looked up from his work. "Enter."

I moved to the front of the desk and saluted.

"At ease, Marine." He stood. "Specter, you've been busy. I heard you fixed a cargo drone at the Receiving Station earlier today."

"Just helping out where I can... sir."

"There just aren't enough Marines to go around and engineers are particularly hard to come by. Things are breaking and we don't have the personnel to fix them. I'm gonna be straight with you. The war effort isn't going as planned. We've lost contact with forward base Phoenix. It may be nothing, just systems breaking down, or it may have fallen to the separatists. Communications and fast travel are offline. I need you to head over there and evaluate the situation. If it's safe, get the damaged systems back online."

"And if it's not safe?" I asked.

"We can't lose Phoenix. If it's under separatist control, then put a squad together and take it back."

<Group Mission: Forward Base Phoenix>

<Recommended Level: 10>

<Bring Forward Base Phoenix Back Online>

<Rewards: 10,000 Experience, 500 Credits, 250 Reputation: Federation Marines>

<Accept - Reject>

I accepted the mission. "Don't worry, Lieutenant. I'll get to the bottom of it."

"Good man. I'll mark the base on your map and put a requisition in for a vehicle for you at the motor pool," he said before sitting back down. "I need you to get there right away."

I turned to leave. Lieutenant Nash called after me when I reached the door.

"Oh, Specter, it could get rough out there. Get yourself in order before you go."

Chapter Thirteen

Get myself in order. It was good advice. So far, I'd stumbled my way through this game, making stupid mistakes. It didn't help that I'd started with someone else's character. If I'd started with my own build, things would have gone much better for me. I would have at least had an idea of how things worked. My new build was working and my shotgun was getting the job done. I wasn't that impressed with the service drone though. Buttons couldn't fight or take damage. I didn't know what it could do besides mark locations on my map. That was useful, but I failed to see the point. It needed a weapon. I had a bomb thrower in my locker. I didn't know how good it was, but it would be better than nothing.

I swung by the barracks and took out the bomb thrower, pistol, and the basic webbing. My old belt was only worth one credit. It wasn't worth the slot it was taking up. I had no plans to use the pistol, so I'd just sell them and free up the space. I took the bomb thrower and touched my wrench to the service drone. From what I had seen so far, that should work to connect it to the drone.

<Weapons cannot be mounted to a service drone.>

"Well shank," I said.

I'd bet dollars to doughnuts Cassandra could tell me what the deal with the drone was. I walked over to her shop, finding her in her usual spot behind the counter.

"I want to mount a bomb thrower on my service drone, but it doesn't work."

She laughed. "It wouldn't work would it? Service drones don't have weapons mounts after all."

"Silly me... So, what can I put on it to help me out?"

"Things like extra storage and scanners."

I sighed. "What kind of scanners can I use with it?"

"I recommend a multipurpose unit. Hang on, I have one here somewhere," she said, stepping out from behind the counter.

She walked over to a bin on the wall and rummaged through it, stopping to examine pieces of machinery as if she were inspecting jewels before picking one out and coming back to the counter.

"This is a good entry-level unit. It will do all kinds of scans. Vegetable, animal, and mineral. Everything you'll need for missions," she said.

"How much?" I asked.

"This unit's a steal at five hundred credits," she said.

"That seems pretty steep."

"It's well worth the cost, considering it scans multiple sources and only takes up one of the drone's two equipment slots."

I pulled up my inventory and checked my credits. I had 273 and I wanted to see about some other equipment as well. "It's a little out of my price range right now. What do you have that's more of a bargain?"

"Well, you could do a single scanner of whatever type you're most interested in. I'd recommend a bio scanner or a system scanner."

"System scanner?"

"For mechanical and electrical systems. Anything from a drone to a vehicle to building wiring."

"How much?"

"They're a hundred credits and take up one slot each."

"What else can I put on it? You said something about extra storage?"

Cassandra pulled a small pouch from behind the counter. "Yep, this is a drone pouch. It has five slots and will run you thirty-five credits. You could also purchase utility systems. For example, a mining unit. Your drone could collect ore on its own. It would need a mineral scanner to function properly."

"Let me have the bio scanner and the bag," I said, producing 135 credits.

I picked up the items and pulled the spanner off my chest. I bent down and touched the spanner to the drone. A progress bar appeared. When it had completed, the scanner and bag disappeared from my hand. An antenna appeared on the back of my drone. I wanted to figure out how to use the bag. When I looked at my inventory, I had another five slots added with squares highlighted in orange. Easy enough. I stood and almost fell back over my drone when I got a look at Cassandra. A green circle had appeared on my minimap where Cassandra was standing. Hers wasn't the only circle either. They were all over my minimap, making it hard to see the map.

"The scanner's working, I take it," she asked.

"The map's a little cluttered."

"Just tell Buttons what you want to display."

"Buttons, can you remove any friendly targets from the map?"

"Processing..." It wiggled its camera and the green dots disappeared.

The last thing was to sell my extra items. Using the console on the counter I sold my pistol, its ammunition, and the webbing. I debated about the bomb thrower. I didn't have a use for it. If I needed one in the future, I could just find another or buy one. Better to get the credits now than carry around gear I couldn't use.

Selling the gear brought me up to 173 credits. Not a lot to work with, but I hoped it would be enough. I knew I wanted a medstick. My next stop was the Medical Center. I picked up a medstick from Dr. Silvers for twenty-five credits. Picking up some extra armor seemed like the best idea. I headed back to the Armor Emporium. I strolled around the shop, perusing the shelves. It was sectioned out by armor type. The mechanized armor on the far right of the shop was interesting and expensive. My lack of funds meant something a little more modest was in order. I looked through the shelves of the medium armor. I had a few possibilities, but I could only buy one piece.

"Having trouble?" Boris asked.

"Yeah, I don't have a lot of credits at the moment, but wanted to pick up some protection."

"Besides chest armor, helmet will give you most protection," he said, walking over to a row of helmets. He took the one off the end and handed it to me.

<Basic Combat Headgear>

<Medium Armor>

<Required Level: 4 - Common>

<Slot: Head>

<Armor: 31>

<Durability: 60/60>

<Cost: 80 Credits>

It reminded me of a hover bike helmet. It offered full face protection with a built-in visor and matched my brigandine vest well. A nice bonus. I produced a credstick and handed it to Boris. The helmet replaced my headset. My heads-up display went down for a moment during the transition. I pulled the helmet off. I couldn't see any of the messages, health bar, or popups if I wasn't wearing some kind of headgear. That meant I could take a break from the system if I needed one. Good to know. I put the helmet back on and pulled up my armor. It was up to ninety. Much better.

Lieutenant Nash wanted me to check out Forward Base Phoenix right away, but the mission said it was level ten. Since I was only level four, I didn't think it would be a good idea to check it out until I got my level up. The mission I was most interested in was Ambush Hunter. Unfortunately, it said it only attacked at night. I didn't know how much longer I had before sundown. From the position of the sun, I guessed a few hours. I had an idea.

"Buttons, how long before sundown?"

The drone did its "processing" shuffle and replied, "Two hours, thirty-seven minutes."

With that much time to waste, I started with Special Delivery. It was low level and should be easy enough to complete. I headed back to the receiving office, sidestepping the delivery drone heading out of the spaceport as I went in. It still had its strained shudder, but it was functioning. I gave Sergeant Hopkins a nod as I passed him. He sneered back at me.

I found the Receiving Office open. Private Barr sat behind the counter, sorting packages and typing on the console.

She didn't look up when I walked over. "I don't have time for you right now. If you want to send a shipment offworld, use the automated services and leave me be."

"Actually, I saw a posting on the board that said you need help delivering mail. I came to offer my services."

She stopped typing and looked me dead in the eye. "You're hired." She reached under the counter and produced packages in a small crate and a stack of letters. "These are all about to pass their scheduled delivery time. Get as many delivered as you can before the deadline. I'll mark the locations on your map."

<Mission Updated: Special Delivery>

<Deliver as much mail as possible before the time expires. Bonus rewards will be awarded for each piece delivered over ten.>

<Accept - Reject>

As soon as I accepted, the timer icon with ten minutes appeared in my HUD and green dots appeared on the map around Port Bax. I picked up the pile of mail off the counter, putting it into my inventory. The crate was in a single inventory slot in my backpack, but it wouldn't do to mess with my inventory on a timed quest. I moved it to my quick draw slot. The spanner disappeared, replaced by a package on my harness. I walked toward the closest dot and quickly figured out it was leading me to Sergeant Hopkins.

He crossed his arms as I approached. "Need directions again? I suppose anywhere away from combat would suit you."

"I have a delivery for you," I said, pulling the package off my chest.

There weren't any names or instructions on it. I handed it to him, wondering if I had the right one. I'm sure if it wasn't right, he wouldn't hesitate to tell me.

Sergeant Hopkins took the package. "I guess it's good you found an assignment more suited to your temperament."

I turned and walked out of the hangar bay. "Always a pleasure, Sergeant."

Chapter Fourteen

The mission was straightforward. Find the person and hand them a package. I decided to deliver all the packages in the military district first. The timer had stopped right after I delivered my third package. I looked at it, wondering why, when I heard a voice behind me.

"Busy?" Faizal asked.

He had a sullen expression. I didn't get the impression he had good news.

"Working on the delivery quest, nothing important."

He nodded. "I paused the timer for you. Didn't want you to miss out on the quest. I don't have time to explain. She'll be here any second."

Why all the mystery? Who was this *she* he was talking about? I wasn't sure why he would bother pausing the quest, either. Did he think I cared about it? If he was back, he could have found Patty or have something to tell me about when I could expect to get transferred to Everafter.

Before I could ask him, a woman in a business suit appeared in front of me. "It looks like it's working. How does it look to you?"

"Yeah, I can see you," I said.

She held up an index finger in my face. "This is him in front of me? Okay... Right." She lowered her finger and looked at me. "I'm Martha Briggs with AGS legal. That's Acuity Gaming Systems. Before we can start, I need you to confirm your name, Colonial Security Number, and date of birth."

"Can you tell me what this is about?"

"After you confirm your identity, then I can speak to you. Failure to comply will result in a forced logout and account ban."

I didn't know why I was speaking to someone from legal. This was a simple mix up that shouldn't take more to fix than a couple of phone calls and printing a shipping label. Then again, Everafter wasn't expecting me anymore. I didn't have an account or resources to get one. I was stuck. I recited my personal information.

"We've been discussing how to handle your situation. I'm being told they're unable to separate your code from the game's files. This leaves us in a precarious situation. With the game going live so soon, we can't delay the release to figure this situation out. We also can't have a ghost in the machine taking up company resources. All our problems would be solved by deactivating your account and we were prepared to do it, when Faizal proposed another option." She shot Faizal a contemptuous look. "If you sign an NDA, that's non-disclosure agreement, and pay the monthly fee you can stay in the game. We're prepared to comp your first month of play to enable you to get your affairs in order."

"Am I going to have a way to contact the outside world?"

"All I need is a signature."

I didn't like the sound of being deactivated. That meant I would be back to taking up space on a hard drive. They would probably forget about me and get back to running their game according to plan. I didn't know how I would pay for the subscription, but signing the paper gave me a month to figure something out. It's not like I could talk to anyone if I was in storage anyway, so the NDA was a moot point.

"Where do I sign?"

A tablet and stylus materialized in her hand. She handed them to me. The document was pages long, written in legalese that hurt my head to read. I scrolled and scrolled, eventually reaching the bottom where there was a place for me to sign. I scribbled my signature.

I passed the pad back. "Okay, so I have some questions."

"I'm sure you do, but I'm not customer service," she scoffed. "Get me out of this thing."

She disappeared. The interaction didn't leave me feeling any better about my situation. With no communications built into the system, I had no way to even get started on correcting my death. It was clear the megacorporation didn't care about me or my rights and would just put me in storage if I caused problems or couldn't pay. There were protections for digital people, but I had no means to act on them.

It's possible I could make friends with someone who could get the ball rolling for me. It wasn't likely. What are the chances I could become close friends with someone, convince them I was stuck in the game, and get them to undertake that kind of hassle in thirty days? Not likely. It would violate the NDA I signed as well. If AGS found out about it, I'd get shelved. I had to accept that I probably had thirty days to live. Once I went in storage, that would be it.

I had forgotten Faizal was standing there until he spoke. "I thought she would give you a few more details. What we know so far is that your files were integrated with the system. Apparently, they were loaded years ago and as the system files were formatted your files were dispersed throughout the entire system. If you didn't know, a human consciousness is about ten petabytes, that's ten thousand terabytes. It's an enormous file. Your files aren't under a single directory. You don't even have a directory. You're just spread out all over the system, just everywhere. Our first idea was to locate your files by searching for their file types. Unfortunately, most of the file types used in virtual reality are the same used in consciousness files. We're still looking at options, but right now it looks like we will have to do a line audit of the entire system. It would take our current staff two or three decades to complete it. If we missed something, you could end up without some memories or come out braindead. Don't worry though, it's not as bad as it sounds."

"How? How is it not as bad as it sounds? You tell me my wife is dead, I'm dead, I'm trapped in a game, and the people that run the game are running out the clock until they can deactivate my account and forget I exist. What am I missing?"

"I'm not saying everything's going to be okay, but I think you can keep your account active, if you want to."

"I don't have any money. I did but it's all gone now. There's no way I can pay the subscription."

"Just hear me out, okay?"

I took a seat on a crate outside a random building. "Let's hear it."

"There are two in-game currencies, credits and medals. To buy game time, players buy medals and purchase the subscription with them, as well as cosmetic items, vehicles, and gear. You get the idea."

I sighed. "I already said I don't have any money, so I can't buy medals."

He continued, ignoring my interruption. "Medals also drop as loot rewards from elite bosses. They aren't guaranteed drops, and the drop rate was designed so the average player couldn't play for free. The calculations were made based on access to elite monsters, factoring in things like spawn rates, player competition, and average play time. Here's the thing," he said with excitement in his eyes, "you aren't restricted by play time. Sleep isn't required in the game. Since you never have to log out, you never have to sleep, which skews the calculations in your favor. I ran some quick numbers, and it looks like if you focus about half of your playtime hunting elites, you should be able to get the medals you need to purchase your game time."

"Okay, so where are these elite things?" I asked.

Faizal bit his lip. "I can't tell you that."

"Why the hell not?"

"I get you're in a tough spot, and I'll help you where I can, but I'm still an employee of AGS. Disclosing game information is against company policy. I could lose my job and you could get deactivated. We have to keep things aboveboard. There is another way you can get medals though. When the game goes live, you can get medals from other players to ease the time hunting. You can auction items at the military surplus store for credits or medals. You can craft items to sell if you build your skills or the elites give the best loot. You should be able to auction for medals or just trade directly if you can find someone to trade with."

"So, I hunt and kill the strongest mobs in the game to get the medals I need for the subscription. Sounds simple enough."

"Simple but not easy. The drop rates for medals depend on the player level compared to the mob level. So, you'll need to find stronger mobs as you level to keep getting the medal drops. The mobs will respawn about every fifteen minutes. If you can find the spawn location, you can farm medals until you out level it. I probably shouldn't have told you that bit of game information, but it's too late now."

"Well, I appreciate the help," I said. "How many medals do I need?"

"Open up your store menu," Faizal said. "It's the one with the currency symbol."

I found the menu and took a look. Inside the store, there were three special offers that were featured at the top. They were for equipment sets, one for each type of armor: Light, medium, and heavy. They came with a weapon and a few extras. I could get any of them for twenty medals. I wondered how much the medium armor set would have helped me up to now. Would I have been invincible to the sarlocs in the basement if I were decked out in full armor? Not that I have any medals to get it with in the first place. I found the game subscription. Fifty medals for one month of play, over a medal a day. There was an option to buy a yearly pass for 550 medals. If I could somehow afford to save up that many medals, I could get a month for free that way. Seemed like a long shot.

"I found it," I said.

"What are you going to do?"

I shook my head. "Doesn't look like I have a choice. I'll see how many medals I can get."

"I better get back. They're going to keep an eye on you for a while to make sure you stick to the NDA, so be careful about what you say," he said, bringing up his tablet. "Good hunting."

Chapter Fifteen

The way I saw it, I had three options. I could embrace my situation, try to get these medals, and continue what kind of life I could until they could figure something out. Even if they could transfer me today, I still didn't have the money to pay for a retirement home. If I wasn't stuck here digitally, I'd be stuck financially. I could do my best to enjoy myself for the next thirty days until they deactivated my account, or I could just give up and log out now.

I'd been feeling isolated and out of place during my time in the game so far. That had to get better. Eventually, people would show up and I wouldn't be on my own anymore. I could make some friends and have some adventures... I could have some kind of life here, even if it wasn't the life I was expecting. It could be good. I wouldn't know it unless I tried. I'd have to get good at the game and build my character to hunt these elites Faizal had told me about. That wasn't right, good wouldn't be enough. I'd have to be the best. All I had to do was come up with fifty medals in the next thirty days. I wasn't going to do that standing around... better get to it.

I looked at the mission timer, expecting it to have expired. It was still stuck with eight minutes and thirty-seven seconds left. I guess I didn't have to rush after all. The mission took me to many of the military buildings I had visited before, Marines on and off duty, as well as the Motor Pool, which was new. When I'd finished with the military district, I made a lap around the civilian district, passing out packages until all the dots on my map were gone. I headed back to the Receiving Office and found Private Barr at the counter.

"How'd you do?" she asked.

"I delivered them all."

"All of them? Wow, with you on the job, I'll be caught up in no time! Check back with me tomorrow if you need more work," she said. "I'll have more packages to deliver."

<Mission Complete: Special Delivery>

<Reward: 150 Experience, 150 Bonus Experience, 60 Credits, 50 Reputation: Federation Marines>

I gave her a nod. "I'll see you tomorrow."

The delivery quest was easy experience, if I could repeat it tomorrow, I would. If I had to hunt the hardest mobs in the game, I needed to level fast. I opened my mission log and looked through it. The other missions I had seemed to be pretty involved. I didn't think I had enough time to complete another one before sundown, but I might be able to finish Local Flavors while looking for the Ambush Hunter. There had to be sarlocs or something wandering around outside the city I could get cooking ingredients from. I already had half the items I needed for my mission, but I wouldn't mind picking up a few more to try out my cooking skill. Before heading outside the wall, I stopped by the Weapons Boutique and bought all the ammo I could afford. It wiped out what credits I had left. I wasn't worried about it. Between completing missions and loot, I should replace those credits in no time.

While I was delivering packages, I'd seen two gates that led outside town. One was in the east wall by the motor pool and the other in the civilian quarter south of the Armor Emporium. The south gate was closest, so I headed for it. I stepped through the gate, getting a glimpse of the world outside Port Bax for the first time since the shuttle landing. The port was on top of a hill in the middle of a grassy savannah. A line of mountains rose to the west.

"Buttons, can you mark creatures on the map?"

"Scanning… Marking target locations."

Several yellow and red dots populated the minimap. Most of them were on the border of the map. I had one yellow dot somewhere in the grass ahead,

I looked down at my service drone. "You have a pretty good range."

"Range hours at the Waepons Boutique are nine hundred to twenty hundred hours."

"Thanks for the info. You're so helpful."

It did a little half step forward and back as if it enjoyed the praise. It brought a question to my mind that I hadn't thought of before. *How sentient is Buttons?* I wasn't sure anyone I had been dealing with here had a mind of their own, but what if they did? What if they had lives in this game. I had no way to know. If I saw Faizal again, I would have to ask him.

I walked into the waist-high grass toward the closest yellow dot. As I approached, I saw a creature's head poke up from the grass. It had light brown fur, big ears, and two horns that curved up from its head. It looked like an antelope. It surprised me to see a familiar animal, but it made sense. As part of terraforming, animals from earth were brought in to create stable ecosystems. Both predators and prey. Of course, the plants and animals inevitably changed over time due to environmental changes. I took aim at the antelope. My finger moved to the trigger. I looked at me with its big doe eyes, chewing on grass. I lowered my shotgun.

I turned to Buttons. "Can you tell if that antelope will help me complete any of my missions?"

"Scanning… Antelope can provide items needed for the mission Local Flavors."

"Can you only show creatures that will help me complete my missions?"

"Processing… targets marked."

The dots on the minimap didn't change. It didn't look like it made a difference, after all.

"All right then," I said, raising my rifle.

I took aim and fired. Blue pixels exploded on the animal's side. The antelope reared back and charged. I fired again, this time missing. I hit again with my third shot as the animal lowered its head. It was trying to hit me with its horns. I jumped to the side, avoiding the strike, and shot as it charged by. Blue pixels shot out from the animal a moment before it dropped to the ground.

I tapped the body with my foot to loot it before moving to the next dot, another antelope. I moved into range and opened fire. The pixelated explosion looked different from normal. Instead of the blue I was used to, it had orange mixed in. The antelope charged. I fired twice more, missing both times before my third shot dropped the antelope.

I looted it and checked my battle log to figure out what happened with that first shot.

<You Critically Hit Antelope for 108 Damage>

I pulled up my character sheet to find my critical stats. Crit chance was two percent with a one hundred percent damage bonus. I liked critical hits... Attachments or up-grades that would improve my crit might come in handy. I'd have to check with Silas when I made it back to town. I looted the antelope.

<Mission Complete: Local Flavors>

The sun set over the savannah. As it descended across the horizon, the stars, and three moons became visible. It looked like art. A beautiful landscape I was currently living in. I wished Patty was here to see it. The moons did a good job lighting up the night. It was more dim than dark. It occurred to me I hadn't planned for sundown. If it had been dark out, I would've had to go back to Port Bax for a flashlight. Luckily for me, I could see without a light source. It might be smart to head back to town now. I could turn in Local Flavors, clear out what little I had in my bags, and make it back with plenty of time to look for the Ambush Hunter. I checked my character sheet to discover I was a sliver away from level five. Hitting my next level was the priority.

I checked my minimap. There were plenty of yellow antelope dots, but I spotted something different. A group of five red dots was moving in my direction from the south. I looked toward the dots, but didn't see anything. I moved out of the path of the red dots and squatted down in the grass. Buttons knelt in the grass beside me. It didn't need to. The grass was already taller than its body. I waited, watching the map as the dots approached. When they were almost on top of me, I heard a chittering kind of whisper as a group of humanoids walked past.

The creatures were short, standing between three and four feet tall, with light gray skin, large eyes, and a wide mouth that seemed to stretch all the way across their faces. They had black hair and wore plain shirts and pants. They were carrying pistols and SMGs. Marine weapons. I didn't know where they got them, but they had made some modifications. The weapons had organic looking growths on them. The weapons radiated bits of blue light that spilled out of crevices in the growths. They moved quietly through the grass, unaware I was crouched a few feet away. Were these the Pangol Colonel Radim had spoken of?

I watched the minimap as their dots disappeared. I didn't know what kind of challenge a fight with these five would pose, but I didn't want to risk not being ready for the Ambush Hunter. The antelope weren't a challenge. As long as I started shooting from maximum range, I could take them out by the time they got to me. I continued moving through the grass from antelope to antelope until I got the message I had been waiting for.

<You have Reached Level Five>

<You have Unlocked Specializations>

I pulled up my character sheet, finding a new tab for specializations. The specializations tab had three trees: Mechanical, Electrical, and Biomechanical. I did a quick scan of the trees. Mechanical buffed my character, Electrical buffed my drone, and Biomechanical made an engineer into a healer. That was interesting, but a healer probably wouldn't be the best build for hunting elites.

Buffing the drone seemed okay, but the trees showed buffs for damage and since Buttons didn't actually do any damage, it didn't make sense to invest into that tree. Maybe that meant I could upgrade my drone. Something to look into. For now, I'd stick to the mechanical tree. I had two choices. Traction Fluid increased my fire rate by 5% and Cross-linking increased player and drone accuracy by 1%. Since I leveled up my skill, I wasn't having a problem hitting enemies. Fire rate seemed the logical choice. I had one point to spend, but wasn't sure if there would be any unexpected consequences with the selection. I decided to wait to assign my point. The stakes were too high to make a stupid mistake.

The specializations I had access to that buffed drone damage made me think I could either upgrade my drone or get a new one. Cassandra had mentioned a battle drone... I wondered if I could get one at level five. I would have to go back to town to do it though. Going back to town meant I might miss the Ambush Hunter, assuming I could find it at all. I would probably have to complete another mission before I could get an upgraded drone, so I might miss out on the hunter if I changed courses now. Then again, some extra firepower could come in handy. I'd been out here for a while and hadn't found the hunter. Staying out until my inventory was full made the most sense. If I hadn't found it by then, I'd head back to see what Cassandra could tell me about the drone.

Chapter Sixteen

I headed in the opposite direction of the Pangol, making quick work of a couple more antelope. My stomach growled. It was an unexpected sensation. The hunger bar on my multimeter was down by a half with an icon beside it. I selected it.

<Hungry: Your hunger icon is depleted by half. Health and Energy restoration are reduced by ten percent.>

That sounded inconvenient, but not a huge deal. I hadn't been taking much damage and my energy bar was still full. My plan was to stay out until I filled my inventory or found the Ambush Hunter. It occurred to me I might be able to use Buttons to speed up this hunt.

"Buttons, can you scan for the Ambush Hunter?"

"Scanning…" Buttons said, turning in a circle. "Unable to locate target: Ambush Hunter."

It was worth a shot. I moved toward the next yellow dot, finding another antelope meandering through the grass. I took aim and fired, scoring a critical hit. My next shot was a second crit. I killed it so fast it had barely moved. Two crits in a row, must be my lucky day. I walked over and looted the antelope.

<Inventory is Full>

That was it, I hadn't found the hunter. I still had enough ammo, but no storage space.

Checking my inventory, I found seventeen chunks of meat in two stacks, a stack of ten and one of seven. I didn't feel like heading back to the city so soon. After all, it was a nice night. I had a camp stove I could use to cook something to eat. I took it out of my inventory and set it up on the ground. It looked like a small gas-powered grill. A small blue flame sprang to life with the push of a button. I took a Hunk of Meat out of my inventory and placed it on the stove. The spinning clock appeared over the meat. I got a message after thirty seconds.

<You have Created Burnt Kabob>

The meat pixelated and turned into three charred looking pieces of meat on a skewer. I pulled it off and gave it a sniff. It smelled... burnt. I took a bite. It didn't taste great either, but it was something to put in my stomach. It brought my hunger icon up by a quarter and got rid of the hunger debuff.

I cooked all the meat, except for the ten I needed for Local Flavors. I put one Hunk of Meat on the stove after another, pulling off burnt kabobs one by one. I got into a rhythm cooking the meat. Taking them off the stove, putting them in my inventory, and getting a chunk of meat for the next cook. When I was on my eleventh piece, I noticed the kabobs could stack in higher numbers than the meat. I was good to know I could free up inventory space with cooking.

I had placed the last kabob in my inventory when I thought I heard rustling in the grass. Standing up, I looked out, seeing the wind gently flowing through the grass.

"Buttons, are you detecting anything around us?"

"Scanning... Five biosigns are approaching from the north."

The minimap showed five dots in the distance. The Pangol must have doubled back. I turned to collect the stove and get out of sight. Not fast enough. The sound of screaming electricity erupted from behind me. I felt the tingling shock of being shot in my back. I jumped to the ground, grabbing my shotgun, and looking at the minimap. The five red dots spread into a half circle behind me. Lasers tore through the grass, streaking overhead. I lay in the dirt, trying to pinpoint an enemy's location. Shad-owy figures silhouetted against the night sky approached through the grass. I pulled the shotgun against my shoulder and took aim at the closest silhouette, placing my finger on the trigger. There was a feline roar, and the figure disappeared, pulled away somewhere out of sight.

The lasers stopped firing. I got to a knee, still aiming, and listened. The Pangol seemed to have lost interest in me and were focused on something else. I didn't see any new dots on the minimap, but now there were four red dots instead of five. I stood, attracting the attention of the closest Pangol. It spun to shoot. Before it could fire, the grass shuddered before a wave rushed toward the Pangol. The creature disappeared into a vortex of swirling grass. Whatever was out there was large and fast. The three remaining Pangol opened fire where their comrade had been standing a moment before.

Something rushed out of the grass, striking the back of my leg. It disappeared back into the grass before I could get a look at it. I watched a fifth of my health disappear. I had a new debuff.

<Hamstrung: Movement Speed is Reduced by Half.>

I had matted down a section of grass while I was making the kabobs. I moved beside the stove. It felt like I was walking through thick mud. I wouldn't be able to run from this fight the way I had run up the stairs from the sarlocs.

I turned in slow circles, trying to spot whatever was out there. The three remaining Pangol were turning back-to-back. They lost all interest in me. I glimpsed a large shadowy figure barely taller than the grass that seemed to be walking on four legs. I couldn't tell what it was. I just knew it wasn't humanoid. It wasn't marked on the minimap. I had no way of telling where it was. I spotted a section of grass that shook. A black cat the size of a tiger burst out of the grass, charging me. Its eyes didn't have pupils, just white orbs with bloodshot veins. It had a metal contraption on its head. I tried to leap out of the way. The hamstrung debuff was doing its job, keeping me from getting away. The cat raked its claws across my legs before disappearing back into the grass. The timer in the hamstrung debuff renewed and my health bar dropped again.

I wasn't prepared for this fight. With a quick shuffle of my inventory, I swapped the spanner on my chest for the medstick. I pulled the medstick off my harness, giving myself a quick shot. The grass shuffled again, this time close to the Pangol. I slapped the medstick back on my chest and fired just as the beast charged from the grass, dragging another Pangol away.

I looked down at Buttons. "If you see any moving grass mark it on the map."

"Scanning…" Buttons said.

My health was down to fifty percent, but climbing slowly from the medstick. A red dot appeared behind me. I spun as fast as I could but couldn't get turned around before I took another hit and the cat disappeared into the grass again. The Pangol fired their lasers after the creature, filling the air all around me with laser fire. This just wasn't working. Between the hamstrung debuff, and the grass, I wasn't going to win this fight. I needed to get rid of one, or both. The camp stove sat at my feet with its blue flame shooting steadily out of the top. I kicked the stove over. The flames licked the grass for a moment before it caught. The fire burned in a circle in the grass. It grew and spread, burning a growing ring in the grass. I realized I hadn't been paying attention to the monster when it attacked me again. My medstick cooldown was done. I gave myself another shot and stepped inside the ring of fire onto charred grass.

I waved a hand at the Pangol. "Hey, come over here."

They didn't seem to understand the words, but they got the idea. They ran over to stand back-to-back with me. I pulled a tube of shells out of my ammo pouch and reloaded my shotgun as I waited for the fire to pick up speed. The hamstrung timer ticked away and my health slowly climbed. I couldn't take more than one more hit. Luckily for me, I didn't see any new dots. Just when I thought the fire scared the cat away, a red dot popped up on my minimap. The cat leapt out of the grass onto the burned grass twenty feet away. Buttons must be able to track it outside of the grass.

It charged again as my hamstrung timer ran out. I stepped to the side, feeling much quicker, and avoided the attack. The Pangol and I opened fire. I missed much more than I had with the antelope. We kept shooting as the cat abandoned its charge, disappearing into the grass again. Its dot disappeared from the minimap. The Pangol beside me chattered, something I couldn't make out. The cat charged out of the grass, attacking the Pangol to my right. The Pangol opened fire first, blasting it with its lasers. I fired the Instant Karma, the rounds exploding into blue pixels on the animal's back. It spun and tackled the last Pangol, biting into the little creature and shaking it back and forth in the air. I stepped forward and kept shooting. It let go of the Pangol, sending it rolling off to my right. It turned toward me, baring its fangs. I fired once more. The monster's face disappeared behind an explosion of blue. The cat dropped.

<Mission: Ambush Hunter: Complete>

Chapter Seventeen

I finished the fight with two rounds in the shotgun and a hair over half-health. If not for the Pangol soaking damage, I would have been killed. Even though they had attacked me to begin with, we ended up on the same side. I didn't know what I should do with them. I didn't want to take them back to Port Bax. For all I knew, there could be some military scientist looking for Pangol to experiment on. I wondered what they would do with their dead. Bury them? Burn them? Did they do anything? Once I looted them, their bodies would probably disappear like the sarlocs in the basement of the Drone Warehouse. I was probably overthinking the whole thing.

"Buttons, can you find the bodies of the dead Pangols?"

"Processing... locations marked."

I looked at the minimap to find four green dots and one yellow. The discrepancy confused me when I realized one of the Pangol was still alive. It was lying in the charred grass.

Its clothes were torn and stained with soot. It lay with its chest raising and lowering slowly, looking peaceful. It didn't seem so monstrous anymore. I knelt beside the creature, unsure what to do. It might wake up on its own if I left it alone or something else might come by and eat it. There was only one thing to do. I pulled the medstick off my harness and injected it.

I took one of the Burnt Kabobs out of my pack and stuck it in the ground, standing up beside the creature before backing away. I walked over to the Ambush Hunter, nudging it with my foot to loot it. A couple items went to my inventory before a message popped up.

<Inventory is Full>

A loot box with some nice items in it opened. I pulled up my inventory to see what else I had. Between the two windows, I had some attachments and armor that might be worth a look.

<Chorym L14 Compensator>

<Level: 5 - Uncommon>

<Attachment: Muzzle Break>

<+1% Critical Hit Chance>

<Range: 40 Meters>

<Durability: 50>

<Value: 25 Credits>

<Napsin DP3>
<Level: 4 - Uncommon>
<Pistol - Bind on Equip>
<+1 Fortitude>
<Damage: 40–70>
<Value: 65 Credits>

<Harper E1>
<Level: 4 - Uncommon>
<Attachment: Laser Sight>
<+7 Damage>
<Value: 32 Credits>

<Oribe Medical Trousers>
<Level: 5 - Rare>
<Light Armor Bind on Equip>
<+4 Fortitude>
<Armor: 65>
<Slot: Legs>
<Durability: 60>
<Value: 136 Credits>

<Grossan P81T>
<Level: 3 - Uncommon>
<Attachment: Scope>

<Accuracy: +6>
<Value: 40 Credits>

<Gromber Barrier Generator>
<Level: 4 - Uncommon>
<Shield Bind on Equip>
<Energy: 20>
<Recharge: 30 Seconds>
<Durability: 45/45>
<Value: 50 Credits>

<Strange Device – Quest Item>

I could equip some of these items. That wouldn't take up backpack space, but I had to have a space free to move them into my inventory to equip them. I found a tuft of fur that wasn't worth anything and got rid of it to make space. I'd start with attachments. I could put two on my shotgun, but I had three to choose from. The scope gave plus six accuracy, the laser sight gave plus seven damage, and the muzzle break increased crit chance by one percent. I had been missing a lot of shots against the Ambush Hunter. It made sense that elites would be harder to hit than normal mobs, so the scope was a no brainer. I liked the crits but a straight damage buff would be more reliable.

Using my spanner, I attached the scope and laser sight to my Instant Karma.

I turned my attention to the pistol. I didn't have a second weapon equipped so I could equip it to free space. There wasn't a reason to use it, but it had a plus one to fortitude. If I could get the bonus just by having it equipped, that would be worth it. I equipped the pistol and checked my stats. Sure enough, my fortitude and hit points had increased. The Oribe Medical Trousers were light armor, so not ideal, but the plus four to fortitude was a big improvement. I equipped them. The BDU pants I had been wearing were only worth one credit, so I dropped them on the ground. That left the Gromber Barrier Generator. It looked like some kind of shield. I wasn't sure what slot it would use. When I equipped it, it went into the class slot I didn't know what to do with and appeared on my side. A glowing light spread out from the barrier generator surrounding my body. When it had covered me completely, it faded. My multimeter had a new purple ring around the outside designated as shield.

The rest wasn't useful to me. Even if I couldn't use it, it would sell for more than the other junk I'd collected. I ended up picking the items with the lowest credit value that I thought I wouldn't need and dropped them before looting the items from the cat. When I looted the Strange Device a message popped up.

<Mission: Ambush Hunter>

<Mission Progress: Acquire Proof of the Ambush Hunter's Demise: Complete>

With the loot sorted, I looked over to discover the Pan-gol was gone, along with the Burnt Kabob I had left for it. A yellow dot on my minimap headed west. I headed back to Port Bax. I could turn in Local Flavors. I really just wanted to take a break.

Parson was behind the counter at Pour Decisions. "Specter, good to see you. What'll it be?"

"I got those cooking ingredients for you."

I took the items out of my inventory and placed them on the counter. Parson took them and placed a metal tin on the counter in their place.

<Mission Complete: Local Flavors>

<Rewards: 50 Experience, 25 Reputation: Port Bax Shopkeepers Union, 10 Credits, C Ration>

"I could use more of these. I can take ten cooking ingredients a day if you can collect them."

"Thanks, Parson. I'll see what I can do. How about a drink?"

"Sure, what'll it be?" he asked.

"I'm in the mood to try something new. Dealer's choice," I said.

I was enjoying the game. I hadn't planned to like it, but it snuck up on me and I was having fun. If Faizal was right, I had a shot at having some kind of life. It wasn't the life I was expecting. I thought I would be enjoying a nice retirement with Patty. Now I had a much more adventurous prospect, if not a preferable one. If I was going to do it, I had to make a strategy. Hunting these tough mobs meant I had to find them first. That meant spending a lot of time outside of town. I needed the skills to survive in the wilderness and the power to take them down. I was going to sit here, dig into all the information I had access to, and come up with a plan. If I could stay alive long enough, one day, maybe, I could be removed from the game and sent to where I was supposed to be.

Message from the author

Thank you for reading! I hope you enjoyed my work. If you did please consider leaving me a review, signing up for my newsletter, or referring this book to a friend. You can use this QR Code for my website, social media, and more.

About the author

Ben grew up in Dahlonega, the biggest small town in the North Georgia mountains. He spent his childhood appreciating nature and, as he grew older, benefited from a wide variety of unusual and exciting experiences. Ben traveled internationally, including Europe and India. He participated in, and won, a martial arts competition, was hit by a ricocheting bullet, and was in a high-speed car chase. He also received a late-night phone call from the secret service, who he hung up on.

Ben appreciates fantasy and sci-fi in all forms, with a particular fondness for shifters. He excels at creative, outside the box thinking combined with a drive toward realism that gives his work a unique feel.